DEADEYE

Written by

Jay Moriarty

and dedicated to everyone
who ever wanted to be a cowboy

Antler
PUBLISHING

DEADEYE

COMMENTS FROM SMART PEOPLE WITH GOOD TASTE!

"DEADEYE is a WINNER!"

"Great story!"

"Great roles!"

"Can't wait to see who plays Deadeye!"

"Comic and touching."

"Timely and timeless."

"Will make a great movie!"

"Best movie I haven't seen!"

"Wonderful film that will also play well in other countries!"

"Didn't want it to end."

"Will make a great series!"

AUTHOR'S FOREWORD

Based On a True Dream

When I was around 8 years-old, a new kid moved into our neighborhood and told us his name was Roy. After about three months, my mother learned from his mother that his name was really Joel. He called himself Roy because his idol was Roy Rogers. You might think the neighborhood kids would rag on him and start calling him something like "Lying Little Prick" or "Bullshit Billy" or even—at least when parents were around—"Joel."

But we didn't. Because we understood perfectly. We just called him Roy and changed our own names to our idols. Who wouldn't rather be called Hopalong, Cisco, Tonto or Wild Bill? Even Mary Sue became Annie Sue, after her idol Annie Oakley. We all wanted to be cowboys or cowgirls when we grew up.

The story you're about to read, if you dare, is not a Western. It's a tribute to Westerns. More specifically, a tribute to the iconic genre of "cowboy shows." Sort of like Don Quixote was a tribute to stories of chivalric knighthood which Cervantes devoured while growing up in 17th Century Spain.

Growing up in 1950s and early 60s America, we learned our morality and developed our goals from watching the ubiquitous TV and movie heroes like Roy, Gene, Hopalong, Cisco, Wild Bill Elliot and The Lone Ranger. As dedicated fans, many of us still recall the sponsors (and even the commercial jingles) of our favorite shows—products like Wonder Bread ("Helps Build Strong Bodies 12 Ways"),

Butternut Bread ("Tut, Tut Nothing But Butternut Bread!") and Gene Autry's favorite chew ("Double your pleasure, double your fun, with Doublemint, Doublemint, Doublemint Gum").

I don't want to spoil the story for you, so I won't say any more about what's in the following pages. But I sincerely hope it's as much fun to read as it was to write. To sum up, I'll simply say it's a tale about courage. The thing Hemingway describes as "Grace under pressure." Or what a cowboy might call "Pluck." It's a story about fighting to make your dreams come true. A story based on a true dream.

PHOTO COURTESY OF KEVIN HOPPS

PROLOGUE

In 1950s America, cowboy shows flooded the TV airwaves. Hopalong Cassidy, Gene Autry, The Lone Ranger, The Cisco Kid, Lash LaRue, Red Ryder and, of course, the acclaimed King of the Cowboys, Roy Rogers—to name a few. The cowboy shows themselves were morality tales where right always trumped wrong and justice always won out.

As a rule, good guys were decked out in white hats and studly duds; while villains donned black hats and grittier getup. The hero and his horse, who would always come when called, were joined at the saddle. Mental and physical toughness plus skill with a weapon were *de rigueur* for a cowboy hero. When necessary, our hero could shoot the gun from a varmint's grip, or singlehandedly take on a handful of gnarly galoots.

At the time, almost every kid in the country wanted to be a cowboy or cowgirl when they grew up. Cowboy hats, rhinestone holsters and toy guns were on every kid's Christmas list. And Richie Wentworth was no exception. From Richie's first day in kindergarten—when he insisted on bringing his Hostess cupcake snack in his Roy Rogers lunch box (the one with Roy, Dale, Trigger and Bullet on the front)—till teenage dating intervened, Richie's dream was to become a cowboy.

iv.

"The hardest thing in the world is
believing in yourself when nobody
else does."

                           ~ Deadeye

FADE IN:

FILM CLIP—OLD COWBOY MOVIE—DAY

A COWBOY HERO on a white horse is racing along an open trail.

CUT TO:

INTERIOR MOVING CAR—DAY

It's 1977. Young lawyer RICHARD WENTWORTH is speeding along a Minneapolis freeway. Richard is around thirty. He has curly, disheveled hair and a fresh, handsome face with the eyes of a dreamer.

EXTERIOR MOVING CAR—DAY

Richard's blue Porsche, classy but unwashed of late, turns off the freeway onto a downtown off-ramp.

EXTERIOR MOVING CAR—DAY

Richard's Porsche moves along a downtown street, then makes a quick turn into an alley marked ONE WAY - DO NOT ENTER.

INTERIOR MOVING CAR—DAY

Tight on Richard's face as he barrels the wrong way down this one-way street.

CUT TO:

FILM CLIP—OLD COWBOY MOVIE—DAY

A Cowboy Hero races full speed on horseback.

CUT TO:

2.

EXTERIOR MOVING CAR—DAY

A van pulls into the alley at the other end; and
RICHARD manages to swerve between the van and the
wall just in time, narrowly avoiding a head-on
collision.

EXTERIOR DOWNTOWN STREET—DAY

Richard's Porsche turns into the Parking Garage
of a huge office building.

INTERIOR BUILDING HALLWAY—DAY

An elevator door opens. Richard, wearing a suit,
tie, wing tip shoes, and carrying his briefcase, exits from the elevator. He moves to a
door marked ATKINS, ROSS & POWERS - LAW OFFICES.
Richard opens the door and enters the office
corridor.

INTERIOR OFFICE CORRIDOR—DAY

Richard passes by a row of five or six office
doors, each guarded by a Secretary—what office
assistants were called in those days. A couple of
the SECRETARIES are busy typing, the others are
chatting from their desks. RITA, a short blonde
secretary with a pixie haircut, stops Richard in
front of his office.

                    RITA
(WITH AN AIR OF IMPORTANCE)
        Oh, Richard. Mr. Atkins wants to see
        you.

                    RICHARD
(NOT OVERLY CONCERNED)

Okay, Rita. Thanks.

Richard moves into his office.

INTERIOR RICHARD'S OFFICE—DAY

He sets his briefcase down, sits at his desk, and looks through a pile of pink phone messages.

SFX: a loud buzz.

                    RICHARD
(PUSHES BUTTON ON HIS INTERCOM)
     Yes?

                ATKINS (VOICE OVER)
     Richard, I'd like to see you for a
     minute in my office.

CUT TO:

FILM CLIP—OLD COWBOY MOVIE—DAY

A Cowboy Hero confronts the VILLAIN in a saloon shootout. The Hero outdraws the Villain and shoots the gun from his hand.

BACK TO:

INTERIOR RICHARD'S OFFICE—DAY

                    RICHARD
(BEAT)
     Be right over, Mr. Atkins.

Richard gets up, subconsciously adjusts his belt, and exits into the office corridor.

4.

INTERIOR OFFICE CORRIDOR—DAY

He walks across the corridor and knocks on a
closed office door.

                    ATKINS (VOICE OVER)
    Come in.

Richard opens the door and steps into Atkins'
office.

INTERIOR ATKINS' OFFICE—DAY

MR. ATKINS, a handsome grey-haired man in his
late 50s, dressed in a vested Brooks Brothers
suit, sits behind his large wooden desk. His
pipe-cleaning kit is spread out on his desk, and
he continues cleaning his pipe while talking to
Richard.

                    ATKINS
(MOTIONS TO CHAIR IN FRONT OF HIS DESK)
    Sit down, Richard.

Richard closes the door, moves to chair and sits.

    Richard, I like you. I always have.
    You're a good worker. You're dedicated.
    You're extremely bright. In fact, when
    we hired you out of law school, you had
    the highest grades of any new man we'd
    ever hired. We had great expectations
    for you—and we still do. But lately...
    Well, I guess it's no secret that your
    work's been dropping off. Now I know
    you've had some personal problems; and
    I hope you're able to get everything
    straightened out. But as your employer,

I have to be concerned with your atti-
tude at work. What you do here has an
effect on the whole firm. That's why
a true professional learns to leave
his personal problems at home. Do you
understand, Richard?

CUT TO:

FILM CLIP—OLD COWBOY MOVIE—DAY

The Hero smacks the Villain square in the jaw and
sends him sprawling.

BACK TO:

INTERIOR ATKINS' OFFICE—DAY

Richard nods in answer to Atkins.

                    ATKINS

I knew your father well, Richard. He
was a first-rate lawyer—a real professional. And I'm sure he wouldn't want
you jeopardizing your career—no matter
what the reason. You understand?

CUT TO:

FILM CLIP—OLD COWBOY MOVIE—DAY

The Hero blocks the Villain's punch, hits the
Villain in the gut, then lands a punch to the
Villain's jaw.

BACK TO:

INTERIOR ATKINS' OFFICE—DAY

6.

Richard nods in answer to Atkins.

                    ATKINS

     Good.

Richard gets up to leave.

          Oh, by the way. If you're concerned
          about the Larkin hearing tomorrow,
          don't be. I talked to Judge Howard last
          night. He's an old friend of mine. Just
          be sure you show up and enter a plea.
          (SMILES) Understand?

                    RICHARD
(TRYING TO HIDE A SURGE OF DISGUST)

          I understand, Mr. Atkins.

INTERIOR OFFICE CORRIDOR—DAY

Richard exits from Atkins' office and moves
across the corridor to his own office.

INTERIOR RICHARD'S OFFICE—DAY

Richard opens his briefcase and begins removing
some files. From the corridor, TOM SYKES spots
Richard and enters Richard's office. Tom, about
Richard's age, also works as a lawyer at Atkins,
Ross & Powers.

                    TOM
(CHECKS BEHIND HIM TO MAKE SURE NO ONE IS
LISTENING)

          Hey, the old man's been looking for
          you.

                    RICHARD

      I just talked to him.

                      TOM

(CURIOUS)

      Yeah?

Tom stares at Richard as if to say "What did he
say?", but Richard's thoughts are wandering.

Tom pops a Tum into his mouth (from the roll he
is holding in his hand); and then, trying to
break the silence, offers a Tum to Richard.

      Want a Tum?

Richard, drawn momentarily from his dream world,
shakes his head "No" to the Tum.

          Richard, uh... Listen, I know things
          have been pretty tough for you lately.
          You know, I, uh, I've been through a
          divorce myself.

                    RICHARD

          Remember how Wild Bill Elliott used to
          wear his guns? So he could cross draw?

Richard mimes a two-handed cross draw.

CUT TO:

Scene from a Bill Elliott movie showing ELLIOTT
cross drawing his guns.

BACK TO:

Richard's office.

8.

                          TOM

        If there's anything I can do to help,
        Richard, just...

                        RICHARD

        And remember how Red Ryder used to hop
        on his horse? From the back?

CUT TO:

Scene from a Red Ryder movie showing Red Ryder
mount his horse with a running leap from behind.

BACK TO: Richard's Office.

                          TOM

(POPS ANOTHER TUM INTO HIS MOUTH)
        Sure you don't want a Tum?

Richard is dreaming.

                        RICHARD

        Tom, did you ever want to be a cowboy?

                          TOM

(FORCED TO CONVERSE ON RICHARD'S TERMS)
        A cowboy? (LAUGHS)

                        RICHARD

        Ridin' through the West from town to
        town, helping set things right.

                          TOM

        Hell, I guess everybody wanted to be a

cowboy at one time or another. Either
that or a pirate. You grow up, though;
and you find out you can't always be
what you want.

(POPS ANOTHER TUM INTO HIS MOUTH)

Besides, life in the Old West wasn't as
glamorous as they show it in the movies.
Things were pretty rough back then.

Richard is standing at his office window, staring
at the cloud formations outside.

RICHARD

Well, at least in those days you could
tell the good guys from the bad guys.

Tight on clouds outside.

INTERIOR DR. MECHLEY'S OFFICE—DAY

Pull back from clouds to show Richard's POV:
He is now lying on a couch staring at the sky
through the window of a high-rise office building. Richard's suit coat is off, lying over the
arm of the couch at his head.

He is in the office of DR. NORBERT L. MECHLEY,
psychiatrist. Mechley, who is seated in a chair
just a few feet from Richard, is fortyish,
bespectacled, with short brown hair thinning
on top. Mechley's semi-mod attire—stylish suit,
flowered shirt and colorful tie—seems to clash
with his short, stocky body, giving him an almost
comical appearance. He sports a neatly-trimmed
beard—so neat that he looks straighter and
stuffier than he would if clean shaven. Mechley
is holding a note pad and pen.

10.

The telephone on Mechley's desk rings. Mechley
moves to the desk and picks up the phone.

                         MECHLEY
          Dr. Mechley speaking. (LOWERS HIS VOICE
          WITH AN EYE ON RICHARD) Oh, hi. Yes,
          he's here. No—just a few minutes late.
          Yeah. Okay, fine. Goodbye. (HANGS UP)

Mechley returns to his chair. Richard stares at
Mechley.

          That was your sister.

                         RICHARD
     (ANNOYED)
          Figured.

                         MECHLEY
          Does it bother you that someone cares
          about you?

                         RICHARD
          Are you kidding? All she cares about is
          her family name.

Mechley doesn't respond.

          Well, you won't have to worry about
          her bothering you anymore, because this
          is our last visit. I promised her I'd
          come here for six sessions, and this is
          number six.

                    MECHLEY

     Frankly, Richard, I think you should
     keep coming—at least for another
     session or two.

                    RICHARD
          (GETS UP AND MOVES TOWARD WINDOW)
     Look, Mechley, I already spilled my
     guts out to you.

Richard stands at the window, hands in pockets.
He stares out at the clouds.

     Remember when we were talking about
     goals last week?

                    MECHLEY

     Yes?

                    RICHARD
          (STILL STARING OUT WINDOW)
     Well, I've been thinking. You know,
     there's only one thing—just one thing—
     I ever really wanted to be.

                    MECHLEY

     What's that?

                    RICHARD

     A cowboy.

                    MECHLEY
          (HIS PROFESSIONALISM KEEPS HIM FROM CHUCKLING)
     A cowboy?

12.

                          RICHARD
(TURNS)
     When I was a kid, I always wanted to be
     a cowboy.

(SMILES EXCITEDLY AS HE REMEMBERS)
     Like Johnny Mack Brown.

CUT TO:

Fight scene from a Johnny Mack Brown movie.

BACK TO: Richard.

                          RICHARD
     Or Hopalong Cassidy.

CUT TO:

Fight scene from a Hopalong Cassidy movie.

BACK TO: Richard.

                          RICHARD
(HIS IMAGINATION BEGINS TO TAKE OVER AS HE
PUNCHES AT THE AIR)
     Or Roy Rogers.

CUT TO: Fight scene from a Roy Rogers movie.

BACK TO: Richard.

Now Richard hums his own fight scene background
music and provides all the other necessary sound
effects as he fiercely fights with an imaginary
gang of outlaws, knocking them all over Mechley's
office.

Not wanting to interfere with his patient's form
of release, Mechley at first stands casually by,
waiting for Richard's childish playing to cease.

But Richard's antics become wilder and wilder.
Finally, Mechley speaks up.

                    MECHLEY
     Okay, Richard, I think that's...
     Let's...Richard, I...

Richard pretends he's been punched and falls
back onto the couch. Using his feet, Roy Rogers'
style, he pushes the imaginary charging outlaw
away.

     Come on, Richard...

Richard hops up from the couch, grabs his suit
coat and throws it up, punching it to the ground.

     You're gonna...

Falling against the other end of the couch,
Richard notices a large teddy bear on the floor
in the corner. Pretending it's an outlaw, he
picks up the bear, wrestles with it, and starts
beating the hell out of it.

                    MECHLEY
(PANICS)
     Oh, no! For God's sake, Richard, Mrs.
     Hiller's teddy bear! If you break
     Snooky, she'll kill herself! But she'll
     kill me first!

Mechley attacks Richard, trying to pull the
teddy bear away. Mechley finally manages to free

the bear; but then Richard grabs Mechley by the collar, cowboy style, and starts a roundhouse swing towards Mechley's face. Mechley, holding the teddy bear, goes limp from shock, anticipating the blow—but Richard's fist stops just a half-inch from Mechley's nose.

                    RICHARD
(TO MECHLEY)

        Lucky for you you're wearing glasses,
        stranger.

INTERIOR COURTROOM—DAY

In tight on JUDGE HOWARD as he moves from the door of his chamber into the courtroom. He is a distinguished-looking man in his late 50s.

            COURT CLERK (VOICE OVER)
        All rise.

Wide shot of the courtroom. There are quite a few SPECTATORS present. Everyone stands. The Judge moves to his bench and sits.

            COURT CLERK (NOW VISIBLE)
        Be seated.

Everyone sits.

        The United States District Court,
        Central District of Minnesota, is now
        in session, the Honorable Morton Howard
        presiding.

                    JUDGE

    This court is now ready to hear
    class action case 24-078, the People
    of Warren County versus the Larkin
    Development Company.

(GLANCES AT FOLDER IN FRONT OF HIM)

    The Defendant is charged with seven
    counts of conspiracy to willfully
    defraud the residents and prospective
    homeowners of Meadow View Estates in
    Warren County. How does the Defendant
    plead?

The Judge glances down at two Larkin Company
VEEPEES who are seated at the Defense table. The
Veepees are middle-aged, dressed in business
suits. Neither received the memo that the Buzz
Cut is out. Next to them, where Richard should be
sitting, is an empty chair.

The door opens in the back of the courtroom and
Richard enters carrying his briefcase. He's
dressed in a business suit and is wearing a pair
of decorative, Western-style cowboy boots. As
he walks up the aisle, the Larkin Veepees turn,
throwing Richard an anxious look. Richard smiles
at them assuredly, and they relax.

                    RICHARD
(TO JUDGE)

    Your Honor, I'm counsel for the
    Defense. May I approach the bench?

                    JUDGE

    Permission granted.

16.

Richard sets his briefcase on the edge of the
Defense table and approaches the Judge. The
PLAINTIFF'S LAWYER, a young, well-dressed black
man, also approaches the bench.

At the bench, Richard speaks in a voice that only
the Judge and the Plaintiff's Lawyer can hear.

                    RICHARD
          Your Honor, my client is guilty.

Surprised, the Judge and the other Lawyer wait
for Richard to say more.

                    JUDGE
     (FINALLY)
          That's all? Just "guilty"?

                    RICHARD
     (THINKS)
          No, make that guilty as sin.

The Plaintiff's Lawyer smiles, thoroughly
puzzled.

                    JUDGE
     (STUNNED)
          Huh?

                    RICHARD
          Judge, those two Larkin Veepees
          (MOTIONS TO THE BUZZ CUTS) admitted to
          me that they've been stealing money
          from homebuyers for years.

The Plaintiff's Lawyer grins broadly, not sure
he's hearing right.

                    JUDGE
(VERY UNEASY)

     Mr. Wentworth, why are you telling me
     this?

                   RICHARD

     Well, Judge, I know the court is inter-
     ested in a fair trial. And letting
     these outlaws go free just wouldn't be
     fair.

Richard turns and moves to the Defense table.
He smiles at the Buzz Cuts as if to say "Don't
worry, it's all taken care of." And they smile
back, confident. Richard takes his briefcase and
walks toward the courtroom door. Angle on his
cowboy boots.

The Judge and the Plaintiff's Lawyer watch,
speechless, as Richard heads down the aisle for
the exit.

              PLAINTIFF'S LAWYER
(STILL SMILING IN DISBELIEF)

     He's crazy!

Tight on Richard as he exits courtroom.

CUT TO: scene from a Lone Ranger movie.
MAN and WOMAN on porch.

              WOMAN (IN MOVIE)
     Who was that masked man?

18.

                    MAN

     I don't know. He didn't even stay
     around to let us thank him.

                   WOMAN
(HOLDING BULLET)

     All he left was this silver bullet.

                    MAN

     Silver bullet?

(TAKES BULLET) (LOOKS UP)

     Martha, that was the Lone Ranger!

Film shows LONE RANGER and TONTO riding off in a
cloud of dust.

EXTERIOR COURT BUILDING—DAY

Richard moves down the steps outside the Court
Building. Angle on his boots. Without stopping,
Richard tosses his briefcase into a litter basket
at the bottom of the steps.

EXTERIOR MINNEAPOLIS SIDEWALKS—DAY

Pleased and relieved, Richard moseys along the
summer sidewalks of downtown Minneapolis. A
variety of angles stress the modern elements of
the city: PEOPLE in a hurry; crowded traffic;
smog; new, taller buildings going up; MEN at work
on the sewer system.

EXTERIOR DOWNTOWN COFFEE SHOP—NIGHT

A neon sign in the window says HAL'S DINER - OPEN
24 HOURS. Richard exits through the door of the
diner and moves out onto the deserted evening
sidewalk. Along with his boots, he is now wearing
Levi's, a Western style shirt, a cowboy hat,
and an authentic-looking two-gun holster set.
His holsters are decorated with red rhinestones
and metal studs; and his authentic-looking play
six-shooters are positioned backwards in his holsters, Bill Elliott style.

Richard is unwrapping a stick of Doublemint
gum. He puts the gum in his mouth and tosses
the wrapper into a litter basket. He stretches,
pats his full belly, and breathes in the cool
night air. Looking a bit awkward in his new duds,

20.

Richard moves down the sidewalk, passing the windows of closed stores.

He notices a mannequin display in one store window, and stops suddenly. He turns to a male mannequin dressed in a summer suit and challenges him.

                    RICHARD
(HANDS HANGING AT SIDES, READY TO DRAW)
     Okay, Bart, go for it.

A beat, then Richard attempts a fast draw. Cross drawing, he fails to get one gun out of the holster and the other gun goes flying from his hand.

He picks up the gun, puts it back in his holster, and prepares to try again. He sets himself in position, arms hanging loose at his sides.

                    RICHARD
(TO MANNEQUIN)
     Make it fast, Bart. It's gonna be your
     last.

Richard tries another cross draw. He gets both guns out all right, but is unsatisfied with the speed. Too slow! He puts his guns back and pre-pares to try again. He stares hard and silent at the mannequin; then, suddenly, Richard draws. This time both guns go flying from his hands.

Disappointed, Richard goes to pick up his guns. He puts one gun in his holster; and as he bends down to pick up the other, he hears a noise and sees a slight movement in the shadows on the sidewalk.

                    RICHARD
      (PICKS UP GUN AND POINTS IT AT THE SHADOWS)
        Okay, come out with your hands up!

A tense beat; then a white-bearded WINO with a
cane moves into the light.

        Hand me that rifle.

The Wino stares, confused, as Richard moves to
him and takes his cane away. Richard examines
the cane as if it were a rifle—turning it over,
checking the accuracy of the sight. He pretends
to empty the rifle's ammunition, then hands the
cane back to the puzzled Wino.

22.

> RICHARD (CONT'D)
>
> Nice rifle you got there, mister. If
> you wanna keep it, you better not let
> me see you around these parts again.
> Now git!

The Wino hobbles off down the street as fast as
he can go; and Richard, pleased with himself,
twirls his gun and puts it back in his holster.

INTERIOR RAILROAD DEPOT—NIGHT

Richard is standing at the ticket window. A crag-
gy-faced old MAN behind the screen is talking to
Richard.

> MAN
>
> Sorry, bud. The next passenger train
> doesn't leave 'til tomorrow at noon.
> Only thing going out of here tonight
> are freight cars.

EXTERIOR TRAIN YARD—NIGHT

Richard moves quietly through the moonlit train
yard. He crosses the tracks and moves alongside a
boxcar.

Suddenly, he notices a WATCHMAN, lantern in hand,
walking in his direction. Richard moves between
two connecting cars to the other side of the
tracks.

The Watchman approaches, stops, holds his lantern
up and checks inside a couple of the cars.
Richard leans quietly against the train, waiting
for the Watchman to pass by.

As the Watchman moves closer, Richard becomes fidgety. He reaches for his guns, accidentally dropping one in the cinders.

The Watchman stops, listening.

Richard, crouched and holding both guns, waits at the edge of a boxcar.

The Watchman starts to move between two cars and across the tracks.

SFX: Train whistle blows.

The Watchman stops, realizing the train is ready to move out, and heads back toward the station.

Relieved, Richard straightens up, puts his guns away, and moves to the side of a boxcar whose sliding door is slightly ajar. Richard opens the door farther and quickly climbs up into the car.

24.

INTERIOR BOXCAR—NIGHT

Richard sits on the floor of the boxcar, his back up against the car wall.

SFX: Train whistle blows again.

                    MALE VOICE (O.S.)
    I wouldn't sit there.

Richard freezes.

He looks up to see a dimly-lit figure sitting atop some boxes at the other end of the car. This is BENNY, an earthy transient in his early twenties. Benny has dark eyes, and dark, shoulder-length hair.

SFX: Train whistle.

                    BENNY
    When the train starts moving, man,
    those pipes will roll down right where
    you are.

For the first time, Richard notices the stacks of large metal pipes directly in front of him. He moves up on top of the boxes in the back, near Benny.

The train starts moving, pulling away from the station.

Angle on the spot where Richard had been sitting. The train picks up speed, there is a jolt, and the heavy metal pipes go crashing down, slamming hard against the side of the boxcar.

Richard gulps, realizing that Benny has just saved his life.

                    RICHARD

(TO BENNY, SINCERELY)

     Thanks.

Benny digs the last crumb from a box of Animal
Crackers, then tosses the box aside. Benny
stretches out, propping his head on his small,
extremely worn suitcase. For the first time,
Richard notices that Benny has a thick, scar-like
mark across the front of his neck.

Seeing that Benny is ready to sack out for the
night, Richard decides to turn in too. He stretches
out, pulling his cowboy hat down over his eyes.

                    RICHARD

     By the way, this train is going west,
     isn't it?

                     BENNY

     Be in Montana by morning.

INTERIOR BOXCAR—MORNING

Richard and Benny are just waking up as the train
pulls to a stop. Benny grabs his suitcase, and
the two move slowly toward the closed boxcar
door.

Suddenly, the door slides open. Richard and Benny
find themselves facing three WORKMEN who have
come to unload the car.

                    RICHARD

     Train robbers!

(DRAWS HIS GUNS)

26.

EXTERIOR BOXCAR—MORNING

                              RICHARD
(TO MEN)

     Okay, drop your guns and reach for the
     sky!

The Workmen look at each other, confused. Richard
jumps down from the car.

The 1st Man, a burly, tattooed animal, speaks
up.

                              1st MAN

     Hey, what is this?

                              RICHARD
(TO BENNY)

     Get their guns.

Benny climbs down from the boxcar, carrying his
suitcase. He is totally bewildered by Richard's
behavior.

                              BENNY

     Guns?

                              2nd MAN

     These drifters are nuttier than
     fruitcakes.

                              1st MAN
(TO OTHER TWO)

     I want Deadeye here all to myself.
     You guys take the hippie.

1st Man moves toward Richard.

                    RICHARD
(POINTS GUN AT 1st MAN, PULLS TRIGGER AND
IMITATES THE SOUND OF A BULLET)
        Ptew!

                    1st MAN
        You ain't too good with your guns,
        Deadeye. Let's see what you can do with
        your fists.

A roundhouse swing from the 1st Man catches
Richard square in the face and he hits the
ground, dropping his guns.

The other two Workmen attack Benny. A brawl
ensues.

While rolling around on the ground, Richard keeps
struggling to reach one of his guns which is
lying nearby. But his attempts are continually
foiled by the 1st Man.

At one point, the tattooed 1st Man gets Richard
in a bear hug, practically squeezes the life
out of him, twirls him around and throws him up
through the open boxcar door. Richard gets up,
though, and springs from the boxcar down onto two
of the three Men.

In the end, both Richard and Benny get pummeled
terribly.

EXTERIOR RAILROAD TRACKS—DAY

Richard and Benny are moving along a seemingly
deserted stretch of railroad tracks.

Both are terribly beaten; and they moan, limp,
stumble, fall and crawl as they move along. Benny
is struggling to carry his suitcase.

                         RICHARD

    You got a name?

                         BENNY

          Benny, man. What's yours?

                         RICHARD
(THINKS)
          Deadeye.

                         BENNY

          Deadeye?

                         DEADEYE

          Yeah. I'm a cowboy.
(BEAT)

          What are you?

                         BENNY

          I guess I'm what you call a tran<u>ch</u>ient.

                         DEADEYE

          Where you headed?

                         BENNY

          Just comin' from Canada, man. Thought
          I'd go to California for a while.

                         DEADEYE

          You put up a good fight back there,
          Benny.

                         BENNY

          Shit! Never was much of a fighter.

30.

                        DEADEYE
          No, really. You've got guts.

Benny stops and sits on the side of the tracks to
rest.

                         BENNY
          Shit.

(MOANS AND GRABS HIS SIDE)
          Feels like my fucking ribs are broken.

                        DEADEYE
(STOPS AND SITS ON THE OTHER SIDE OF THE TRACKS)
          Benny, how would you like to be a
          cowboy?

                         BENNY
          Huh?

                        DEADEYE
          I could use a good sidekick. How'd you
          like to be my sidekick?

Benny still isn't sure what to make of Deadeye.

                         BENNY
          Shit, I don't know nothin' about being
          no fucking cowboy.

                        DEADEYE
          I could teach you.

                    BENNY

Say, what do you do, anyway? I mean, if
you're a cowboy, why ain't you out on a
ranch or something?

                   DEADEYE

I'm not a ranch type cowboy. I'm a
cowboy like Johnny Mack Brown. Or Buck
Jones. Or Bill Elliott.

                    BENNY

         Who?

                   DEADEYE
(INCREDULOUS)

         Who? Are you kidding?

Benny stares, not sure if he should be embarrassed at his ignorance.

    You know, Johnny Mack Brown, Bill
    Elliott—in the movies.

                    BENNY

Movies? Shit, I never go to movies.

                   DEADEYE

What about when you were a kid? Didn't
you watch television?

                    BENNY

Never had no TV.

32.

                        DEADEYE

        No TV? How did you ever make it through
        childhood?

Benny lowers his chin and shrugs. He takes a
wrinkled pack of regular Camels from his shirt
pocket and removes the last cigarette.

                         BENNY

        I'd offer you a cigarette, but this is
        my last one. We can share it if you
        want.

                        DEADEYE
(ALMOST OFFENDED)

        Cowboys don't smoke. It's not good for
        you.

Benny lights up.

        If you want to be a cowboy, you've got
        to get rid of those cigarettes. That's
        your first lesson.

Benny takes a deep puff and exhales.

                         BENNY

        I don't wanna be no cowboy.

Benny crumples his empty Camel pack and tosses
it.

                        DEADEYE
(GETS UP AND STARTS MOVING ALONG THE TRACKS
AGAIN)

        Yeah, Deadeye and Benny. Deadeye and

Benny. Not bad. Sounds as good as
Hopalong and Gabby, anyway. Or Roy and
Dale. Or... Gene Autry and Frog.

Deadeye has moved a short distance up the tracks.

Benny gets up, picks up his suitcase, and crosses
to Deadeye's side of the tracks.

The two limp along, Deadeye up ahead.

Benny takes a final puff from his cigarette stub,
then flicks it across the tracks.

EXTERIOR ROAD TO RIDING STABLES—DAY

Deadeye and Benny stand at the intersection of
a highway and a dirt road. The dirt road winds
up through a group of corrals. Deadeye looks up
at a hanging wooden sign that says LAZY K RIDING
STABLES.

DEADEYE

This must be the place.

BENNY

(INTENDING TO CONTINUE DOWN THE HIGHWAY)

Well, I'll, uh, I'll see you, man.

Deadeye picks up Benny's suitcase and starts up
the dirt road.

DEADEYE

Remember, keep your knees in, and just
the balls of your feet in the stirrups.

BENNY

Hey, man... I...Wait a minute...

34.

                        DEADEYE
          And don't jerk the reins too tight or
          he'll buck.

                         BENNY
(CALLS)

          Deadeye!

Deadeye turns at the mention of his name.

          Listen, no offense, man. But I, uh, I
          don't wanna ride no horse.

                        DEADEYE
          Come on, don't worry. Just watch me.

Deadeye turns and continues up the road.

Benny stands watching Deadeye. Benny has never
been a leader, and he hasn't yet learned how to
say "No." Besides, he's a bit intrigued by the
fact that someone is actually showing some interest in him.

To date, Benny has never had a real friend.

EXTERIOR RIDING STABLES—DAY

Deadeye and Benny are standing outside of a barn
and corral complex, waiting for horses to be
brought to them. Two wiry WRANGLERS are manning
the stables, bringing the horses around and
helping riders to mount.

The 1st Wrangler helps a GIRL mount a large
horse, and then the Girl and a MALE COMPANION,
already mounted, ride off down a dirt trail
towards a wooded area.

Noticing Deadeye, the 1st Wrangler moves to the
2nd Wrangler.

                    1st WRANGLER
(IN A LOW VOICE)
     Check that dude.

Both smile.

                    2nd WRANGLER
     He's even got his guns in backwards.

                    1st WRANGLER
     I've got just the mount for him.

(SMILES DEVIOUSLY)

     Loco.

INTERIOR BARN—DAY

1st Wrangler enters and approaches a large white
horse tied inside a stall. The horse starts.

                    1st WRANGLER
     Whoa, Loco. Easy, you sonovabitch!

The Wrangler unties Loco and attempts to lead
him from the barn. The horse resists—whinnying,
kicking and moving sideways. In his movement, the
horse steps on the Wrangler's foot.

                    1st WRANGLER
(YELLS)
     You goddam cocksuckin' glue factory reject!

(KICKS THE HORSE'S RUMP AS HARD AS HE CAN)
The horse jumps. The Wrangler lifts his leg and
kicks the horse again, in the same spot.

(JERKS REINS)

> You ever step on my foot again, I'll
> kick your goddam ass right off!

EXTERIOR BARN—DAY

The 1st Wrangler brings Loco around to where Deadeye and Benny are waiting. Benny is already mounted on a large brown horse. The 2nd Wrangler is standing next to Deadeye.

2nd WRANGLER
(TO 1ST WRANGLER, GESTURING TO DEADEYE)

> He wants to know if we got any golden
> palominos.

1st WRANGLER

Golden palominos?

DEADEYE

Yeah, you know, like Trigger.

1st WRANGLER
(MOVES TO DEADEYE)

> We aint got no golden palominos,
> pardner; but you ain't gonna find a
> better hoss than this here stallion.

(HOLDS LOCO'S REINS AND MOTIONS FOR DEADEYE TO MOUNT)

Deadeye checks the big white horse and nods his approval. Deadeye clumsily attempts to climb up into the saddle. Loco bucks and Deadeye ends up on the ground. The Wranglers exchange smiles.

                    1st WRANGLER
(TO DEADEYE)
     He's a mite skittish today. Don't mind
     that, though. You can handle 'im.

The 1st Wrangler holds Loco steady as Deadeye
gets up from the ground. Deadeye attempts to
mount again. This time he manages to arrange
himself upright in the saddle. The Wrangler hands
Deadeye the reins.

                     DEADEYE
(LEANS OVER AND PATS LOCO'S NECK)
     Good boy.

At this, Loco tears off, with Deadeye awkwardly
holding on for dear life.

Benny's horse follows at a gallop.

The two Wranglers watch, laughing, as Deadeye and
Loco race wildly across an open field toward a
meadow.

                    2nd WRANGLER
(LAUGHING, WITH A TOUCH OF CONCERN)
     That dude's gonna kill himself.

                    1st WRANGLER
(SMILING BROADLY)
     I'll get him.

He jumps on a nearby horse and races out after
Deadeye.

HORSEBACK CHASE—DAY

As Deadeye races full speed across the field
and through the meadow, he imagines that he is
displaying his trick riding prowess, like movie
cowboys Yakima Canutt or Ken Maynard.

Deadeye is bouncing and leaning all over the
saddle, seemingly unaware of the very real danger
of falling off his horse and bashing his head in.

Benny, still unsure of why or how he's become involved in all this, is nevertheless instinctively following Deadeye, bouncing up and down in the saddle as his horse gallops in Deadeye's tracks.

The 1st Wrangler is now racing across the field, whipping with the reins and using his spurs to make his horse go faster.

Deadeye's white stallion seems to be moving like the wind now, flying across the meadow.

The Wrangler catches and passes Benny.

40.

With the Wrangler not far behind, Deadeye and his
horse approach a ridge near the end of the meadow.

Deadeye's horse races up over the ridge and
straight for a wooden fence which separates the
stable property from open country.

                    DEADEYE
          (ENCOURAGING HIS HORSE)
     Hyah! Hyah!

Running at full speed, Deadeye's horse leaps up
and over the fence as Deadeye holds on tight,
almost sailing from the saddle.

As the Wrangler approaches the fence, his face
registers concern.

He is debating whether or not to attempt the
jump. He quickly decides, though; and, spurring
his horse, the Wrangler charges and just barely
clears the fence.

Deadeye, now in open country, with mountains
stretching in the distance, appears in a LONG
SHOT to be just what he thinks he is: an old-
style cowboy hero, galloping freely across the
Western plains.

Benny and his horse reach the wooden fence; and
Benny wisely manages to lead his horse to a
nearby gate. Leaning from the saddle, Benny opens
the gate and rides his horse through. Benny then
gallops out into the open country, following
Deadeye and the Wrangler.

The Wrangler is gaining on Deadeye.

Deadeye reaches a creek and his horse jumps
across.

Seconds later the Wrangler reaches the creek and
jumps across.

As Deadeye's horse races under a tree, Deadeye reaches up and grabs onto an overhanging branch, and his horse continues on.

Benny reaches the creek. His horse attempts to jump across, but trips; and Benny lands in the water. Benny gets up, dripping wet.

                         BENNY

     Shit!

Hanging from the tree branch with both hands, Deadeye struggles to pull himself up onto the branch. The best he can do to conceal himself, however, is to simply wrap both legs up around the branch.

The Wrangler, galloping hard after Deadeye, approaches the tree. As he passes under the over-hanging branch, Deadeye drops straight down on the unsuspecting Wrangler. The Wrangler flies from his horse and hits the ground hard, smacking the back of his head on an extended tree root.

Deadeye springs up, ready to slug it out with the Wrangler. But the Wrangler just lies under the tree, unconscious.

Benny rides up as Deadeye is checking out the Wrangler.

                         DEADEYE
(TO BENNY)

     He's out cold.

Benny is breathing hard, soaked.

     What happened to you?

42.

                         BENNY
              Aw, I fell in that fucking creek.
              Goddam horse tripped.

Deadeye looks toward a cluster of rocks and
WHISTLES loudly.

                         DEADEYE
              Star! C'mere, boy!

                         BENNY
(CONFUSED)
              What're you doing now, man?

                         DEADEYE
              I think Star's up in those rocks
              somewhere.

                         BENNY
              Star?

                         DEADEYE
              Yeah, my horse.

Starts toward rocks.

                         BENNY
              Shit, man! Forget that wild horse! You
              can ride back with me, c'mon.

                         DEADEYE
              Ride back? We're not riding back to
              anywhere. I'm gonna get Star and then
              we're all heading west.

BENNY

What're you talking about, man?

We can't take off with these fucking
horses.

Deadeye moves up to the rocks.

(CALLS AFTER DEADEYE)

Besides, man, I gotta get my suitcase.

CLUSTER OF ROCKS—DAY

Deadeye is climbing over some huge boulders
looking for the white stallion.

DEADEYE

(WHISTLES)

Here, Star!

(WHISTLES)

Here, boy!

Deadeye spots the horse move behind a large rock.
Deadeye scurries up on top of the rock and moves
slowly to the edge. He looks over the edge and
finds himself standing directly above the white
stallion.

Deadeye takes aim and drops from the rock, with
his legs spread wide apart, intending to land
on the horse's saddle. The horse hears Deadeye
coming, though, and moves quickly. Deadeye lands
hard on the ground, lucky not to break both legs.

The stallion attempts to run off, but finds
itself walled in by rocks on three sides. The
only exit is blocked by Deadeye.

44.

The horse turns and starts for the exit, expect-
ing Deadeye to move out of the way; but Deadeye
doesn't budge.

                         DEADEYE
          Easy, Star. Easy. Back, boy. Calm down
          now.

The horse whinnies threateningly.

The horse rears up, attempting to scare Deadeye
out of the way. But Deadeye, faced with being
trampled, still won't move.

          Listen, Star. I know what you want.
          You're just like me. You wanna be free.
          You wanna live. You wanna roam. You
          want adventure. You're no stable horse.
          You're not happy being penned up in a
          corral all day.

The horse moves restlessly, but almost seems to
be listening to Deadeye's oratory.

          Listen, boy, you stick with me and I
          promise you: You'll never have to stay
          cooped up in a corral again. We'll roam
          the West together. We'll ride the wind.

Benny, on horseback, approaches behind Deadeye
and stops.

          We'll go where we wanna go, do what we
          wanna do. And we'll always be on the side
          of justice—doing what's right, helping
          people in need. Deadeye and Star! We'll
          be famous all over the West! Like Roy
          Rogers and Trigger! Or Gene Autry and
          Champ! Or The Lone Ranger and Silver!

(BEAT)

> Come with me, Star. I need you. We need
> each other.

Benny watches in amazement as the horse seems to
calm down.

Deadeye approaches the stallion, takes the reins,
looks the horse in the eyes while patting the
side of his neck, then kisses him.

Star whinnies, and Deadeye mounts. Star rears
back in celebration, like Silver, and then heads
out, crossing Benny's path.

DEADEYE

> Hi yo, Star! Away!

(TO BENNY)

> C'mon, Benny! We're heading west!

Benny's horse seems to get caught up in the excitement, and trots out quickly after Deadeye and Star.

OPEN COUNTRY—DAY

Deadeye and Benny on horseback.

BENNY

(RELUCTANT)

> Jeesuz, man, this is crazy! I mean, my
> fucking suitcase is back at that ranch!

DEADEYE

> Leave it!

46.

                    BENNY
    But everything I own is in it!

                    DEADEYE
    You've got no use for a suitcase now.
    You're a cowboy!

Deadeye and Benny gallop out across the wide open
land, with the setting sun in their eyes, and
"Red River Valley" playing over the scene.

EXTERIOR TOWN—DAY

Deadeye and Benny, on horseback, amble into an
average-size Montana town. They ride along Main
Street, passing a variety of colorful store
fronts—Drug Store, Laundry, Hardware, Bank, and
a cocktail lounge called THE HIDEOUT. The town is
fairly modern, with paved roads, parked cars, and
some automobile traffic. PEOPLE in the town are
dressed in modern 1977 Western garb.

Deadeye and Benny have the only horses in sight,
and some PEDESTRIANS stop to stare at the two
strangers.

As they pass by AL'S PAWN SHOP, Deadeye notices
a classy, red and white Western-style guitar
hanging in the pawn shop window.

Deadeye and Benny bring their horses to a halt
in front of a fairly large food market; and they
dismount and tie their horses to a metal pole
alongside the market.

INTERIOR MARKET—DAY

Benny, pushing a shopping cart, follows Deadeye
around the store, while Deadeye picks out various
items—bacon, beans, shaving cream, razor blades—
and puts them in the basket. As they pass the
Animal Crackers, Benny grabs several boxes and
puts them in the shopping cart.

At the checkout stand, Deadeye picks up some
Doublemint gum. Benny grabs a couple packs of
Camels and places them with the rest of the
supplies.

Deadeye quietly looks at Benny, shakes his head
"No" to the cigarettes, and hands the Camels to
the CASHIER, a heavy-set man in a dirty white
apron, who puts them back on the cigarette stand.

As the Cashier bags the last of the groceries,
Benny—unseen by Deadeye or the Cashier—sneaks a
pack of Camels from the cigarette stand and slips
the cigarettes inside his shirt.

EXTERIOR PAWN SHOP—DAY

Through the window of AL'S PAWN SHOP, we see a
hand take the red and white Western-style guitar
from its hanging place in the window.

Seconds later Deadeye and Benny exit from the
pawn shop. Deadeye is carrying the guitar and
an instruction booklet, and Benny is carrying a
small package.

AT THEIR HORSES—DAY

                         BENNY

          Man, I don't know why you insisted on
          buying me this fucking harmonica. I
          can't play one of these things.

                         DEADEYE

          I can't play the guitar either. We'll
          learn. Even Tex Ritter had to start
          somewhere.

Benny stuffs his harmonica package into his saddlebag, and Deadeye uses the thick strap attached
to his guitar to tie the guitar to Star's saddle.

EXTERIOR "THE HIDEOUT"—DAY

Deadeye and Benny enter THE HIDEOUT, a bar and
cocktail lounge.

INTERIOR "THE HIDEOUT"—DAY

Deadeye and Benny enter. It's a fairly nice
lounge, with a local, country-western flavor.
A bulbous-nosed DRUNK is sitting at the bar,
sipping from a glass of beer; and a few other
local MEN are seated at tables, chatting.

Deadeye and Benny approach the bar. The
BARTENDER, a small, balding man, moves to
Deadeye.

                    BARTENDER
        Wha'dya gonna have?

                    BENNY
        I'll have a draught.

                    DEADEYE
    (SHAKES HIS HEAD "NO" TO BENNY'S ORDER)
    (TO BARTENDER)
        Give us two sarsaparillas.

                    BARTENDER
    (SURPRISED)
        Sarsaparilla?

50.

                              DEADEYE
          Yeah, sarsaparilla. Haven't you ever heard
          of sarsaparilla? It's like root beer.

                              BENNY
          I don't like root beer.

                              BARTENDER
          We ain't got no root beer.

                              BENNY
          I want a draught, man.

                              DEADEYE
          Do you have any milk?

                              BARTENDER
          Milk? Yeah, we got milk.

                              DEADEYE
          Then make it two milks.

The Bartender moves to get the milk.

                              BENNY
          (TO DEADEYE—QUIET, BUT INTENSE)
              Hey, man. What is this? Why can't I
              have a fucking beer?

                              DEADEYE
          Cowboys like us drink sarsaparilla...or
          milk.

                    BENNY

     I told you before, man. I ain't no
     cowboy!

The Bartender returns and sets two glasses of
milk on the bar.

                    BARTENDER

     Here you are—cow juice for two.

The Drunk sitting at the bar looks up momentarily, then looks back at his beer.

                    DEADEYE

(TO BENNY)

     Did you see that fella laughing at us,
     Benny?

                    BENNY

(LOOKS AROUND)

     What're you talking about?

                    DEADEYE

     That fella at the bar there.

(NODS TO DRUNK)

                    BENNY

     Whad'ya mean, man, he ain't laughing at
     us.

                    DEADEYE

     He's laughing at us because we ordered milk.
     We're gonna have to teach him a lesson.

52.

Deadeye takes his glass of milk and moves to the
Drunk.

What's so funny, mister?

                    DRUNK
(TURNS SLOWLY)
    You talking to me?

                    DEADEYE
    You know you oughta drink milk your-
    self, pardner. It's good for you. Here,
    try some.

Deadeye empties his milk glass in the Drunk's
face. As the Drunk sputters, Deadeye pushes him—
and the Drunk and his bar stool go crashing to
the floor.

Deadeye quickly turns around, just in time to stop
an imaginary varmint charging from behind, sending
the invisible fellow sprawling across the bar.

The other Men in the bar watch, and gradually
move out of the way, as Deadeye initiates and
carries out an imaginary bar room brawl, fighting
off at least a dozen imaginary no-count cowhands,
while Deadeye hums his own background fight scene
music.

Falling backwards over tables, throwing chairs
and beer glasses, Deadeye is single-handedly
wrecking the hell out of the place.

The Bartender panics.

                    BARTENDER
    Hey, what're you doing? Stop that!

But he's afraid to approach Deadeye alone.

Somebody get the Sheriff!

A MAN exits.

INTERIOR JAIL CELL—DAY

Deadeye is sitting on a bottom bunk inside a
jail cell. He still has his hat, but his guns are
gone.

INTERIOR SHERIFF'S OFFICE—DAY

The DEPUTY Sheriff, a plump, lethargic-look-
ing man who has almost outgrown his uniform,
is sitting at a desk filling out a report. The
Bartender from THE HIDEOUT is standing at the
desk.

DEPUTY

What d'ya mean he was fighting with
himself?

BARTENDER

Well, he was. He was fighting with
himself.

DEPUTY
(SETS PEN DOWN)

Now, George, how the shit can somebody
fight with himself?

BARTENDER

Well, he went over and threw milk in
Harvey Wilson's face, and pushed Harvey
on his ass. Then he started smashing

chairs and wrecking my whole damn
place!

                    DEPUTY

Did you say he threw milk in Harvey
Wilson's face?

                    BARTENDER

Yeah.

                    DEPUTY
(SHOCKED)

You mean Harvey was drinking milk?

                    BARTENDER

No, that rowdy loon who busted up my
place was drinking milk.

                    DEPUTY
(EVEN MORE CONFUSED)

You mean he got blammed on milk?

INTERIOR JAIL CELL—DAY

Sitting on a jail cell bunk, Deadeye glances up
at the barred window in the back of his cell
and flashes on an idea. He gets up, goes to the
window, and WHISTLES loudly through the bars.

    He WHISTLES again and again, but
    nothing happens.

                    MALE VOICE (O.S.)
Whistling for your horse?

Deadeye turns and spots the speaker, a COLLEGE
KID of about nineteen, sitting on the bottom bunk
in the next cell. The Kid has fairly long hair, a
scraggly moustache, and is wearing a short-sleeve
University of Minnesota sweatshirt.

Sitting on the top bunk, with legs dangling
down over his friend's head, is ANOTHER COLLEGE
STUDENT. He has curly blonde hair and is wearing
a tank top shirt that says MEMBER U.S. OLYMPIC
DRINKING TEAM.

                    DEADEYE

        Yeah. I guess he can't hear me.

                  SWEATSHIRT
    (SMILES AT DEADEYE'S ANSWER)

        You mean you've really got a horse out
        there?

                    DEADEYE

        Sure. I'm a cowboy. My name's Deadeye.
        My horse's name is Star.

                  SWEATSHIRT
    (PLAYING ALONG)

        Yeah? What did they throw you in here
        for, Deadeye?

                    DEADEYE

        Aw, I was teaching some varmints a
        lesson over at the saloon. What are you
        in for?

56.

                         TANK TOP
Out-of-state plates.

                        SWEATSHIRT
(EXPLAINS)
     We got stopped for going ten miles over
     the limit. Guess that's how the cops
     get their kicks around here.

                         DEADEYE
(NOTICING MINNESOTA SWEATSHIRT)
     You go to Minnesota?

                        SWEATSHIRT
     Yeah. This'll be my third year.

                         DEADEYE
     I went to law school there.

                        SWEATSHIRT
     No kidding? Are you from Minnesota?

                         DEADEYE
     Yeah, Minneapolis.

                        SWEATSHIRT
     No kidding? That's where we're from!
     Whereabouts in Minneapolis?

                         DEADEYE
     Well, I grew up in Monford Heights.

                    SWEATSHIRT

Monford Heights? Hey, that's a really
ritzy area. You must be loaded.

                    TANK TOP

Did you say you went to law school?

                    DEADEYE

Yeah.

                    TANK TOP

Why did you quit?

                    DEADEYE

I didn't quit. I passed the bar.
Practiced for a while in Minneapolis.

(THINKS)

Then one day I realized what I really
wanted to be was a cowboy. So now I'm a
cowboy.

Sweatshirt and Tank Top smile, not sure whether
Deadeye is putting them on or if he's a bit
crazy. Either way, they're starting to dig him.

                    SWEATSHIRT

Far out.

                    TANK TOP

You think you can spring us from this
dungeon, Deadeye?

58.

Keys RATTLE in the door which separates the jail
cell corridor from the Sheriff's Office. The
door opens and in walks the Deputy, carrying
Deadeye's guitar.

The Deputy approaches Deadeye's cell.

                    DEPUTY
          Kid named Benny brought this for you.

                    DEADEYE
(SMILES, TO COLLEGE KIDS)
          Benny's my sidekick.

(TO DEPUTY)
          Is Benny out there now? Tell him I want
          to see him.

                    DEPUTY
          Sorry, no visitors.

                    DEADEYE
          I just wanna talk to him for a minute.

Deputy passes Deadeye's guitar through the bars.

                    DEPUTY
          Listen, buddy, you're lucky I'm bring-
          ing you this guitar. If the Sheriff was
          here, he wouldn't even allow that. He
          ain't a music lover like me.

                    DEADEYE
          If I can't have a visitor, at least let
          me make a phone call.

Deputy pauses.

                    DEADEYE (CONT'D)
(INSISTING)

     The law says I have a right to make a
     phone call.

                    SWEATSHIRT
(TO DEPUTY)

     You better listen to Deadeye here. He's
     a lawyer.

                    DEPUTY

Yeah, and I'm a two-headed goat.

                    DEADEYE

     You're gonna be a two-headed goat
     without a badge when I tell the judge
     you wouldn't let me make a phone call.

Deputy stares at Deadeye.

INTERIOR SHERIFF'S OFFICE—DAY

The door leading to the jail cell corridor opens
and Deadeye comes walking out, with the Deputy
behind him.

Benny is standing in the office.

                    DEPUTY
(TO DEADEYE)

     You wanna make one phone call, okay.
     There's the phone.

(POINTS TO A PAY PHONE ON THE WALL)

60.

Deadeye moves to the phone, stops and looks at
the Deputy.

                    DEPUTY
     The law doesn't say I have to loan you
     a dime.

Deadeye digs into his pocket and finds a dime. He
puts it in the phone and dials O. Beat.

                    DEADEYE
     Operator, would you please connect me
     with the Sheriff's Office?

Deadeye re-deposits his dime. The phone on the
Sheriff's desk across the room rings.

The Deputy, uncertain, moves to the phone.

                    DEPUTY
(ANSWERS PHONE)
     Sheriff's Office.

                    DEADEYE
     Hello, I'd like to speak to Benny.

Smiling, Benny moves to the phone. The Deputy,
feeling outsmarted, reluctantly hands the phone
to Benny.

                    BENNY
     Hello?

                    DEADEYE
     Benny, this is Deadeye. How you doing?

                    BENNY
(A BIT PUZZLED)
     Oh, I'm fine, man. How're you doing?

                    DEADEYE
     Fine. Thanks for bringing my guitar.

                    BENNY
     Oh, well I thought you might want it to
     keep you company, you know.

The Deputy SIGHS at the ridiculous nature of the
situation, folds his arms and leans back against
the wall near Benny.

     Besides, man, I didn't want nobody to
     steal it off your horse.

                    DEADEYE
     Benny, take the gun from the Deputy's
     holster and toss it to me.

Before the Deputy realizes what's happening,
Benny grabs the gun and tosses it to Deadeye.
Deadeye catches the gun and holds it on the
Deputy.

                    DEADEYE
(INTO PHONE)
     Thanks a lot, Benny. Bye.

(HANGS UP)

                    DEPUTY
     Hey, now wait just a damn minute, here.

62.

                    DEADEYE
        Sorry, Mr. Deputy.

Deadeye holds the gun on the Deputy and motions
toward the door which leads to the jail cell.

        Move.

                    DEPUTY
(MOVES RELUCTANTLY TOWARDS DOOR)
        You boys are gonna be in a load of
        trouble for this. You know that, don't
        you?

INTERIOR JAIL CELL CORRIDOR—DAY

The door opens and the Deputy comes through, fol-
lowed by Deadeye.

                    DEADEYE
(TO DEPUTY)
        Open that cell.

(MOTIONS TO CELL HOLDING THE TWO COLLEGE
STUDENTS)
The Deputy opens the cell and the two Kids, sur-
prised, jump from their bunks.

                    DEADEYE
(TO DEPUTY)
        Really hate to do this, Mr. Deputy.

Deadeye moves the Deputy to the cell where
Deadeye was and shoves him in. Deadeye quickly
grabs his guitar from the cell bunk and then
closes the door on the Deputy.

Deadeye moves toward the exit door.

> DEADEYE
>
> (TO COLLEGE KIDS)
>
> Let's go!

Sweatshirt and Tank Top, elated, hurry after
Deadeye.

> DEPUTY
>
> Hey, come on now! Have a heart! Don't
> leave me in here! What am I gonna tell
> the Sheriff?

> SWEATSHIRT
>
> (YELLS EXCITEDLY)
>
> Tell him 'Deadeye was here!'

EXTERIOR SHERIFF'S OFFICE—DAY

Background: High-spirited escape music.

Deadeye, Benny and the two College Kids come
running out of the Sheriff's Office and onto the
sidewalk. Deadeye has his toy guns back on, and
his guitar is strapped on his back. Tank Top is
carrying a set of car keys.

Star and Benny's horse are standing right there
where Benny left them, tied to a NO PARKING sign.
Deadeye and Benny grab their horses and mount,
as Sweatshirt and Tank Top jump into their car,
a beat-up green VW bug with a sun roof, which
is parked directly in front of the Sheriff's
Office.

                    SWEATSHIRT
(YELLING TO DEADEYE AND BENNY)
     Yee-hah! Race you to Wyoming!

Deadeye and Benny gallop out of town on
horseback.

EXTERIOR HIGHWAY—DAY

Deadeye and Benny are galloping swiftly and
excitedly along the highway leading out of town.

From behind comes the green VW. Tank Top is
driving, and Sweatshirt is hanging out through
the sun roof, whooping it up. When the College
Kids catch up with Deadeye and Benny, they honk
their horn and wave wildly.

Deadeye waves back, then breaks off the highway
and cuts across the open field towards the mountains beyond. Benny follows.

As the VW pulls away, Sweatshirt cheers wildly.

                    SWEATSHIRT
     Deadeye and Benny! Whoo-eee!

Deadeye and Benny head out on horseback across
the open country.

EXTERIOR ROAD TO RIDING STABLES—DAY

Angle on the hanging wooden sign that says LAZY
K RIDING STABLES.

Pull back to show the lower, side section of a
fairly new station wagon. We see only the two
wheels and the bottom half of the car's left
side, dirty and soiled from traveling, as we
follow the car up the dirt road to the stables.

Suddenly the car stops. The driver's door opens
and out steps a pair of black WING TIP SHOES,
topped with cuffed pants.

EXTERIOR CAMPFIRE—NIGHT

Deadeye and Benny have camped for the night. They are seated around a campfire. Deadeye is holding his guitar and reading from the open instruction booklet in front of him.

Benny is stretched out on the ground, munching on some Animal Crackers.

                         DEADEYE
(AWKWARDLY STRUMMING GUITAR)

         G...G... (TO BENNY) Does that sound
         like a G?

Benny shrugs.

Deadeye attempts to re-tune the bottom string.

         The hardest thing about playing these
         things is getting 'em tuned.

(BEGINS STRUMMING AGAIN, WHILE SAYING THE CHORDS)

         G...G...G... C...C... Back to G...

(ATTEMPTING TO PLAY AND SING, WHILE STUDYING THE
OPEN BOOKLET IN FRONT OF HIM)

         From this valley they say you are

         go... go...C...going...C... We will
         miss...

(SWITCHES TO G, STRUGGLING TO HOLD HIS FINGERS ON
THE RIGHT STRINGS)

         ...miss your bright eyes and your sweet
         D7...

Boy, you know it's hard to concentrate
on the words and the chords at the same
time.

(STUDIES AND ATTEMPTS TO STRUM CHORDS AS HE
TALKS)

Why don't you get your harmonica,
Benny?

                    BENNY

Man, I can't play no musical
instruments.

                    DEADEYE

Have you ever tried?

                    BENNY

No.

                    DEADEYE

Then how do you know you can't?

Benny puts another Animal Cracker in his mouth,
ignoring Deadeye's request.

                    BENNY
(HOLDING UP BOX OF ANIMAL CRACKERS)

Want one?

                    DEADEYE

Got any lions?

Benny crawls to Deadeye and holds up the box.
Deadeye stops strumming his guitar and searches
for a lion.

68.

                    DEADEYE (CONT'D)
          Lions are my favorite.

He finds one and holds it up in the campfire light.

          They're small, but they're brave. You
          know what I mean?

Deadeye bites the head off, as Benny moves back
to where he was.

          What's your favorite?

                         BENNY
          Favorite what?

                         DEADEYE
          Favorite Animal Cracker.

                         BENNY
          Shit, I never even thought about the
          shapes. I just eat 'em 'cause they
          taste good.

Deadeye eats the rest of his lion.

                         DEADEYE
          You know, I've been meaning to tell
          you, Benny. You're gonna have to clean
          up your language.

                         BENNY
          What do you mean?

                         DEADEYE
          I mean you're gonna have to stop cussing.

                    BENNY

Cussing?

                   DEADEYE

Yeah. You know, you're gonna have to
stop using those four-letter words you
always use.

                    BENNY

You mean like "shit"? And "fuck"?

                   DEADEYE

Yeah.

                    BENNY

Shit, man, that's just the way people talk.

                   DEADEYE

That's not the way cowboys like us
talk. If you have to say something, say
"shoot" or "shucks." Or "dangit!" Or if
you're really mad, say "goldangit!" Or
"dadblammit!"

                    BENNY

Shit, I ain't...

The word "shit" hangs there, and Benny's eyes
meet Deadeye's reprimanding stare. To avoid a
confrontation, Benny alters his language.

     I mean, shoot, I told you ten fu...
     (STOPS AND SIGHS) I told you ten times,
     man, I ain't no cowboy.

                         DEADEYE
          You'll learn. I'll start breaking you
          in tomorrow.

Benny sighs and doesn't answer.

Deadeye goes back to studying and attempting to
strum his guitar.

          Where are you from, Benny?

                         BENNY
          North Carolina—town called Buck Creek.
          It's in the Smokey Mountains.

                         DEADEYE
          Does your family still live there?

                         BENNY
          Ain't got no family, man. Just my ma.
          My old man ran off 'fore I was born.

Throws a twig in the fire.

          I left Buck Creek when I was fourteen—
          six years ago. Been hitching around
          ever since.

                         DEADEYE
          Have you ever been back to see your mother?

                         BENNY
          Naw. Thought about it before. But shit,
          she... I mean, shoot, she probably
          ain't even there anymore. She never
          liked me much, anyway. Always said I
          was a stone around her neck.

Deadeye looks over at the scar on Benny's neck.
Since he's got Benny talking, this might be a
good time to ask him about it.

                    DEADEYE

     How'd you get that scar on your neck,
     Benny?

                     BENNY
(LOWERS CHIN)

     Aw, it happened when I was a kid.

Deadeye waits for Benny to say more, but he
doesn't. Benny obviously doesn't want to talk
about it.

Deadeye goes back to studying his guitar.

                    DEADEYE
(STRUMMING AWKWARDLY AND ATTEMPTING TO SING)

     Come and sit by my side if you lo
     ...love me, do not has... (PAUSES TO
     SWITCH CHORDS) hasten to bid me (PAUSES
     AGAIN TO SWITCH) Adieu...

As Deadeye is singing, Benny takes a pack of cigarettes from inside his shirt.

He contemplates taking one out, then realizes
what Deadeye would say. He checks Deadeye, then
stands up and nonchalantly moves toward the brush
behind Deadeye, bootlegging the cigarettes.

     But remember the Red River Valley...
     Valley...and the cow...cowboy that
     lo... (TO BENNY) You going to get your
     harmonica?

BENNY
(CONCEALING CIGARETTES)

No. I've, uh, I've gotta take a dump.

Benny moves into the brush.

EXTERIOR BRUSH—NIGHT

Benny positions himself at the base of a tree
trunk, surrounded by a thick group of bushes, and
joyfully lights up.

DEADEYE (O.S.)

Hey, Benny?

Benny's cigarette is tight between his lips.

Benny?

Benny quickly removes the cigarette from his
lips, dropping a lighted ash on his shirt in the
process.

BENNY
(WHISPERING TO HIMSELF, AS HE BEATS OUT THE
ASH)

Shit!

DEADEYE (O.S.)

Hey, Benny, you okay?

BENNY

Uh, yeah. Yeah, I'm okay.

(GRUNTS, PRETENDING HE'S RELIEVING HIMSELF)

                    DEADEYE (O.S.)

          Hey, I'm gonna sing "Red River Valley"
          all the way through. Listen and tell me
          what you think. Okay?

                         BENNY
          (QUICKLY BLOWING SMOKE FROM HIS MOUTH SO HE
          CAN ANSWER)

              Yeah, okay, Deadeye.

          As Deadeye, O.S., clumsily strums his out-of-
          tune guitar and sings "Red River Valley," Benny
          relaxes against the tree trunk, smoking his ciga-
          rette, thinking intense, faraway thoughts.

                    DEADEYE (SINGING, O.S.)

          From this valley they say you are going,

          We will miss your bright eyes and sweet
          smile.

          For they say you are taking the sunshine

          That has brightened our pathway awhile.

          Come and sit by my side if you love me,

          Do not hasten to bid me adieu.

          But remember the Red River Valley,

          And the cowboy that loved you so true.

          (STOPS SINGING AND STRUMMING)

              Well, what did you think?

          Benny, dreaming, doesn't hear Deadeye.

          There is movement in the brush, and Deadeye's
          voice is closer now.

              Benny?

74.

Benny is startled, realizing Deadeye is coming. He quickly stubs out the butt, coughing on the smoke from his cigarette.

Deadeye, now only a few yards away, spots Benny and moves on camera.

                    DEADEYE

     Oh, there you are. Well, what did you
     think of my guitar playing?

Benny quickly covers his mouth and bends over, coughing uncontrollably from the smoke he inhaled.

Deadeye thinks Benny is ribbing him.

                    DEADEYE
(SHEEPISHLY)

     Aw, come on now, Benny. It wasn't _that_
     bad!

EXTERIOR HIGHWAY—DAY

Deadeye and Benny, on horseback, are ambling alongside a highway leading out of a town. Benny is wearing a cowboy hat and a single gun and holster similar to Deadeye's.

                    DEADEYE
(PLEASED)

     Now you look like a cowboy.

                    BENNY

     I feel like an idiot.

DISSOLVE TO:

EXTERIOR OPEN ROAD—DAY

Deadeye and Benny are riding alongside a long, straight highway which stretches like a tightrope across the open land.

Up ahead is a large green sign with white, iridescent letters, bearing the image of a cowboy astride a bucking bronco. They stop as they reach the sign, which says: WELCOME TO BIG, WONDERFUL WYOMING.

                    DEADEYE

    Yahoo! Get along little dogies!

Deadeye pats Star's neck and gazes out across the airy plains of Wyoming. Star whinnies approvingly.

                    DEADEYE

    Hand me the map, Benny.

Benny hands Deadeye a gas station map of Wyoming. Deadeye, still mounted, opens the map and studies it. A car speeds by on the highway. Benny takes a drink from his canteen.

    Hey, look here, Benny. (POINTING TO
    MAP) A town called Red River. Red
    River, Wyoming. It's not far, either.
    According to this map (LOOKS UP AND
    POINTS), it should be right over there
    a ways.

76.

Deadeye folds map and hands it back to Benny.

(TO BENNY)

> Well, faithful sidekick, let's hit the
> trail. I've got a feeling Red River
> is gonna be the site of our first big
> adventure.

Deadeye and Star veer away from the highway,
galloping off across the plains; and Benny, still
a bit uncomfortable in his new cowboy attire,
follows.

DISSOLVE TO:

EXTERIOR PLAINS—DAY

Deadeye and Benny on horseback. Dry land, hot
sun.

DEADEYE

> One of the first things you have to do,
> Benny, is name your horse.

BENNY

> Why does it have to have a name?

DEADEYE
(AMAZED AT BENNY'S IGNORANCE)

> Are you kidding? All cowboys name their
> horses.

BENNY

> Why did you name your horse "Star"?

                    DEADEYE

          I thought up that name when I was a
          kid. Good name for a horse, don't you
          think?

                    BENNY

          Well, sh... Shoot, man, I don't know no
          horses' names.

                    DEADEYE

          Just look at your horse and try to
          think of a name. What's he look like?

Benny examines his horse's long, brown body and
sloped, flat skull with big, ugly eyes.

                    BENNY

          He looks like a lizard.

                                        DISSOLVE TO:

EXTERIOR PLAINS—DAY

Deadeye and Benny crossing the dry plains on
horseback.

                    BENNY

          Who's Jingles?

                    DEADEYE

          He was Wild Bill Hickok's sidekick. He
          used to do it all the time. Now come
          on, try it again. And this time yell it
          with some feeling.

78.

Deadeye gallops off ahead of Benny. Benny sighs,
but follows orders.

                    BENNY
(YELLS CEREMONIOUSLY)
     Hey, Deadeye, wait for me!

And gallops after Deadeye.

                              DISSOLVE TO:

EXTERIOR PLAINS—DAY

Deadeye and Benny, on horseback, come to a stop.

                    DEADEYE
     Good, good. I think you've got it.
     Let's try it one more time.

                    BENNY
(CEREMONIOUSLY)
     Oh-h-h, Deadeye...

                    DEADEYE
     Oh-h-h, Benny...

          DEADEYE AND BENNY (TOGETHER)
(LAUGHING, CISCO AND PANCHO STYLE, TO THE
TUNE OF "TUT, TUT, NOTHING BUT BUTTERNUT
BREAD")
     Ha ha, ha ha, ha ha ha!

And they ride off.

                              DISSOLVE TO:

EXTERIOR PLAINS—DAY

Benny is racing along on his horse. Deadeye is chasing him on Star. Deadeye catches up with Benny and jumps him. They both go sprawling to the ground.

                              DISSOLVE TO:

EXTERIOR PLAINS—DAY

Benny is galloping on his horse and Deadeye is chasing him on Star. Deadeye catches up with Benny, rides alongside, and again jumps him. They both fall hard to the ground. Deadeye rolls over and jumps up quickly, as if ready to fight. Benny, sore and bruised, rises slowly to a sitting position.

                     DEADEYE

      You think you've got it?

                     BENNY

      When is it my turn to jump you?

                              DISSOLVE TO:

EXTERIOR PLAINS—DAY

Deadeye and Benny are galloping along. Benny rides alongside Deadeye, preparing to jump. But as he springs at Deadeye, Deadeye quickly leans straight back, lying on Star at a 180° angle, and Benny goes flying over Deadeye and Star, landing hard on the ground.

Deadeye circles back and rides up next to Benny, who is trying to pick himself up off the ground. Benny gives Deadeye a disgusted look.

80.

                        DEADEYE
(SMILING)
        That's what you do when somebody tries
        to jump you.

                                    DISSOLVE TO:

EXTERIOR PLAINS—DAY

Deadeye and Benny are ambling along on horseback.
The sun is high and the heat is scorching. Benny
wipes the perspiration from his forehead, then
takes a drink from his canteen.

                                    DISSOLVE TO:

EXTERIOR PLAINS—DAY

Deadeye, Benny and their horses are sweating
profusely. They approach some brush, stop, and
Deadeye and Benny dismount.

Benny takes his hat off and rubs his hand back
through his sticky hair.

Deadeye wipes his brow, removes the canteen
from Benny's horse, and goes about watering the
horses. He pours some water in his hand while
Star laps it up.

                        BENNY
(RUBBING HIS CROTCH AND THE INSIDES OF HIS
THIGHS)
        Man, I feel like a walking saddle sore.

Deadeye pours some water into his hand for
Benny's horse.

                    DEADEYE
(AS BENNY'S HORSE LAPS IT UP)
          Easy, Lizard. Not too fast.

Benny sits on the ground fanning himself with his
hat.

Deadeye takes a drink from the canteen and places
it back on Benny's horse. Deadeye takes out a box
of Animal Crackers from Benny's saddlebag and
feeds some crackers to each horse. He finds a
lion and eats it himself.

                    BENNY
          Man, I don't think I've ever been so
          tuckered in my whole life.

Deadeye kneels on the dry desert ground and draws
a circle with a stick.

                    DEADEYE
          I'll show you how to tell what time it
          is.

(LOOKS UP AT THE SUN)

          Let's see. The sun's gonna be setting
          over there (POINTS), so that's west.
          North is that way (LOOKS), and south is
          that way. (LOOKS)

Deadeye marks a line across the circle on the
ground, and scratches an "N" at one end and an
"S" at the other. Then he forces the stick to
stand up in the center of the circle. The stick
casts a lined shadow.

    See there. Sundial. North is twelve
    o'clock. You just check where the
    shadow points, and you know what time
    it is. (TURNS TO BENNY) It's now two
    o'clock.

Camera moves in tight on the sundial, with the
shadow at two o'clock. The sundial remains on the
screen, with the shadow moving slowly, through
the following Dissolves.

                              DISSOLVE TO:

EXTERIOR PLAINS—DAY

Deadeye and Benny, hot and sore, are plugging
across the seemingly endless desert plains.

                              DISSOLVE TO:

EXTERIOR PLAINS—DAY

The sundial shadow stops at five o'clock and
fades as Deadeye and Benny walk their horses to
some nearby rocks. Both Deadeye and Benny are
exhausted and suffering from the heat.

They stop at the rocks. Benny takes the canteen
from his horse, removes the cap, and presses the
canteen to his parched lips. He throws his head
back all the way, then lowers it in disgust.

                         BENNY

     Fuck! I mean shit! I mean shoot, we're
     outta water, man!

Benny slams the canteen against the rocks. He
leans back against the rocks and gazes out across
the plains.

     Are you sure you know where we're
     going, man?

                         DEADEYE

     We're going to Red River.

Both are breathing heavily. Benny takes a pack of
Camels from his shirt and puts one in his mouth.

                    DEADEYE
     Benny, what are you doing?

Benny gets out his matches.

     Where did you get those cigarettes?

Deadeye moves to Benny.

                    BENNY
(DEFIANT)
          They're mine.

                    DEADEYE
          Sorry, Benny, but I can't let you do
          that.

Deadeye grabs the pack of cigarettes from Benny's
hand and the cigarette from Benny's mouth, crumples them, and tosses them up over the rocks.

                    BENNY
(FUMING)
          Okay, that does it, man! Goddammit,
          I've had it! Can't smoke, can't drink
          a goddam beer, can't say fuck or shit—
          end up lost on some goddam fucking
          desert... Man, I can't take it no more.
          I ain't no cowboy! Can't you under-
          stand that? I AIN'T NO FUCKING COWBOY!!
          Look at me, man. I'm a nothin'. I'm a
          useless, wasted nobody, and that's all
          I'll ever be. I may be dumb, man, but I
          ain't crazy. At least I know what I am.
          And if we ever get outta here alive,
          I'm going back to traveling alone. You

find some other asshole to be your
'sidekick.'

Just then there is HISSING and a RATTLE. They
look down to see a rattlesnake. They both freeze.

                    DEADEYE
(SPEAKING SLOWLY TO BENNY)

    Hold it. Don't move.

Deadeye cautiously removes his gun from his
holster and carefully aims it at the snake.

(PULLS TRIGGER AND MAKES SHOOTING NOISE)

    Ptew!

The snake flies at Benny and strikes him in the
lower leg.

Deadeye quickly grabs the snake by the tail and
begins swinging it around in circles over his
head. He bashes the head of the snake against
the rocks a number of times, then sends the snake
sailing up over the rocks.

Benny is on the ground, holding his leg. He rolls
his pants up to reveal the bite.

Deadeye quickly removes his belt and kneels next
to Benny.

                    DEADEYE

    Just hold your leg steady.

Deadeye tightens the belt around Benny's calf,
above the bite.

    I can't understand it. I hit that
    rattler right between the eyes.

                         BENNY
(MOCKING)
     Yeah—'Deadeye.'

Deadeye takes a razor blade from his saddlebag.
Kneeling next to Benny, Deadeye prepares to make
a cut over the wound.

                         BENNY
(TENSE)
     You sure you know what you're doing?

                         DEADEYE
     Just hold still. Don't move your leg.

Deadeye slowly slices an "X" over Benny's bite.
He sucks the blood from Benny's leg and spits the
bright red fluid onto the dry ground. He repeats
this five times. Benny watches his blood hit the
dirt.

                         BENNY
     Hey, man, you're gonna drain me dry.

EXTERIOR OPEN COUNTRY—DAY

The sun is setting. Benny is sitting bent over on
his horse. Deadeye is walking, leading the two
horses. Deadeye stops. Up ahead is the silhouette
of a single prairie house.

                         DEADEYE
     It's a house all right. We're in luck.

INTERIOR PRAIRIE HOUSE BEDROOM—NIGHT

Benny is lying on a bed with his wounded leg exposed. A very pretty dark-haired WOMAN (TESSA) is at the bedside. She is chewing on some roots, and then applying the quid to Benny's wound.

Deadeye and a PRAIRIE MAN, a big-boned fellow with weathered skin and bad teeth, are standing in the room a few feet away.

                    PRAIRIE MAN
(EXPLAINING TO DEADEYE)
     The Injuns call it "jewel weed." Best
     thing in the world for snake bite.

Benny observes appreciatively as the Woman applies the medicine.

     Tessa's a full-blooded Crow. Her pappy
     and grandpappy were both tribe shaman.

EXTERIOR PRAIRIE HOUSE PORCH—NIGHT

Deadeye is seated on the steps of the long wooden porch, strumming his guitar and singing. The Prairie Man is seated on the porch swing, also strumming an old folk guitar and singing. His two children, a dark-haired GIRL of about five and a BOY of about nine, are seated on either side, smiling wide-eyed. The children of this prairie family are shy; but, like their father and Tessa, their Indian mother, they are thrilled to have visitors.

Deadeye strums the guitar like a beginner, but the Prairie Man's guitar picking is great. They are in the middle of "Red River Valley."

DEADEYE AND PRAIRIE MAN

(SINGING)

>   Come and sit by my side if you love me,
>
>   Do not hasten to bid me adieu.
>
>   But remember the Red River Valley,
>
>   And the cowboy that loved you so true.

As they finish they all laugh, proud of their music. Benny and Tessa come through the front door and onto the porch. Benny has a blanket wrapped around him. Tessa helps Benny to a nearby wicker chair.

                    PRAIRIE MAN
(REFERRING TO BENNY)

     He's looking spry as a spring chicken
     now.

                      TESSA

     The swelling is almost gone.

Tessa moves to a chair and sits.

                    PRAIRIE MAN

     Well, there's nothing better for curin'
     ills than some good range music.

                     DEADEYE

     I'll get your harmonica, Benny.

Deadeye turns to the saddlebags hanging on the
porch rail and removes Benny's harmonica.

                    PRAIRIE MAN

     You got a mouth harp?

                      BENNY

     I can't play it.

Deadeye hands the harmonica to Benny.

                    PRAIRIE MAN

     I used to be able to blow one of those
     things.

Benny hands the harmonica to the Prairie Man.

90.

The Prairie Man blows on it a bit, checking the tune. Then he stands up and plays a lively rendition of "Turkey in the Straw," dancing a barnyard jig while blowing away.

The others begin clapping hands in time; and a rush of complete merriment takes over. Benny is particularly impressed and surprised by the music coming from the harmonica.

When the Prairie Man finishes his song and dance, the others clap and cheer. Benny's face lights up in wide-eyed exhilaration. He is happy. Perhaps the happiest he's been.

EXTERIOR SHERIFF'S OFFICE—DAY

This is the same Sheriff's Office and jail from which Deadeye escaped with Sweatshirt and Tank Top.

A low angle shot picks up the lower left side of a station wagon as it pulls up in front of the Sheriff's Office and stops. The driver's door opens and out steps a pair of black WING TIP SHOES.

EXTERIOR PLAINS (SWEAT LODGE)—DAY

The sun is high and the air is hot. Deadeye and the Prairie Man are kneeling at an outdoor campfire, heating large flat rocks. Behind the campfire is an Indian Sweat Lodge. The Sweat Lodge consists of a mound of dried mud and thatched branches, about four feet high, with a small, square cave-like entrance leading into the ground.

Nearby is an old wood panel truck which belongs to the Prairie Man.·

Using sticks made for the purpose, the Prairie Man picks up one of the hot flat rocks and carries it to the Sweat Lodge.

INTERIOR SWEAT LODGE—DAY

Benny is seated behind a low, flat oven-like structure inside the steamy, cramped quarters of the Sweat Lodge. Benny is sitting naked, with knees pressed up against his chest. His chin rests on his knees, and his arms are wrapped around the front of his legs.

The Prairie Man appears at the entrance and, using his sticks, places the hot rock next to the other rocks on the oven in front of Benny.

EXTERIOR SWEAT LODGE—DAY

                    PRAIRIE MAN
        Bring me one of them water buckets,
        Deadeye.

Deadeye goes to the panel truck and removes a wooden bucket full of water from the back. He carries it to the Prairie Man.

INTERIOR SWEAT LODGE—DAY

The Prairie Man appears at the entrance, reaches in and dumps a bucket of water on the hot stones in front of Benny. A cloud of steam jumps from the rocks and envelops Benny's naked body.

EXTERIOR SWEAT LODGE—DAY

Deadeye and the Prairie Man are relaxing near the panel truck.

                    PRAIRIE MAN

          Tessa's pappy built it here after he
          left the reservation. Sweat Lodge is an
          old Injun custom. All the Plains Injuns
          had 'em.

The Prairie Man's voice continues as a VOICE
OVER as we CUT TO:

INTERIOR SWEAT LODGE—DAY

Benny is sitting enveloped in a dry mist of
cleansing steam, sweat pouring from his open
pores.

                 PRAIRIE MAN (VOICE OVER)

          Used 'em for curin' all sorts of mal-
          adies. Injuns believed when you was
          sick, you had evil spirits in you. They
          used the Sweat Lodge to chase away the
          evil spirits. Sweat out the poison.

EXTERIOR SWEAT LODGE—DAY

Deadeye and the Prairie Man stand at the Sweat
Lodge entrance, each holding a bucket of water.
At their feet are a couple more water-filled
buckets.

Benny emerges from the Sweat Lodge and takes a
deep breath of dry desert air. He stands straight
and naked, hands cupped over his crotch, as
Deadeye and the Prairie Man each pour a bucket of
cold water over Benny's head.

Benny's entire body tingles with glee as Benny
yelps and runs out across the wide open desert
plains.

Deadeye and the Prairie Man each pick up another bucket of water and chase Benny's naked form across the plains.

A variety of shots show Deadeye and the Prairie Man, both laughing uncontrollably, as they chase Benny.

At one point the Prairie Man tosses water at Benny, but the water misses and hits Deadeye. Deadeye then chases the Prairie Man, finally dousing him with a bucket of water.

EXTERIOR SWEAT LODGE—DAY

Deadeye and Benny are standing in back of the panel truck. Benny has an Indian blanket wrapped around him. Deadeye is putting empty buckets into the truck. The Prairie Man is in the background, removing heated stones from the Sweat Lodge and placing them in the outdoor campfire.

                         DEADEYE
(TO BENNY)

        You look just like an Indian in that
        blanket.

                         BENNY

        You know, somebody told me once that my
        old man was part Indian.

(THINKS)

        I don't think it's true, though.

                         DEADEYE
(SUDDENLY LIGHTS UP)

                    DEADEYE (CONT'D)
Benny, that's it! Of course... No
wonder you can't get the hang of being
a cowboy! You're an Indian!

                    BENNY
(CONSIDERS THIS)
Ahh...

                    DEADEYE
Sure! Why didn't we think of that
before? A lot of guys had Indian
sidekicks—the Lone Ranger, Yancy
Derringer... Yeah! That'll work:
That'll work great! You can be my
Indian sidekick!

                    BENNY
(NOT SURE)
Shit, man...

(THINKS)
Can Indians smoke?

                    DEADEYE
One thing for sure—Indians don't cuss.

Their smiles meet.

EXTERIOR PRAIRIE HOUSE—LATE AFTERNOON

Harmonica music—the tune of "Red River Valley"—is
coming from inside the prairie house. Someone is
learning how to play.

Deadeye and the prairie family Boy are in the yard in front of the house. Deadeye has his guns on, and the Boy is wearing Benny's gun and holster set and cowboy hat. Deadeye is teaching the Boy some of the finer points of drawing a gun.

                    DEADEYE

    I can either cross draw like this...
    (CROSS DRAWS) See? (PUTS GUNS BACK)

    Or if I just wanna take out one gun, I
    go like this... (TURNS HIS RIGHT HAND
    INWARD AND DRAWS HIS RIGHT GUN)

    See?

Deadeye helps the Boy arrange his single gun and holster low on his hip.

                    DEADEYE

    You wear it low like this; so when you
    draw (TAKES BOY'S HAND AND PLACES IT
    OVER THE GUN HANDLE), your hand's right
    there. See?

Deadeye is facing the Boy.

                    DEADEYE

    Okay, draw.

They both draw their guns.

Deadeye's cross draw is surprisingly smooth and quick; and he even twirls his guns before setting them back in his holsters. He's been practicing. The Boy's draw is adequate.

    Good, good! You're gonna be the fastest
    kid on the prairie.

Close to a TIGHT SHOT of the house, where the harmonica music is coming from.

> DEADEYE (O.S.)
> Okay, let's try it again. Hold your
> hand a little lower this time. Relax...

INTERIOR PRAIRIE HOUSE—NIGHT

Deadeye, Benny and the prairie family are seated at the dinner table. They are all eating heartily. The meal is obviously the best Deadeye and Benny have had in a long time.

> DEADEYE
> (EATING THE MAIN COURSE)
> This is delicious, Tessa!

Tessa, thrilled at having the opportunity to display her cooking talents to appreciative guests, smiles and shyly nods her thanks.

> BENNY
> Sure is, ma'am.

> PRAIRIE MAN
> It's rabbit meat and wild berries.
> Injuns call it "pemmican."

They all continue to eat, too busy enjoying the meal to talk.

EXTERIOR PRAIRIE HOUSE—NIGHT

The whole group is gathered on the front porch listening to Benny play a rendition of "Red

River Valley" on the harmonica. Deadeye and the Prairie Man are strumming their guitars to back him up; but Benny, even though his playing is a bit rough, is stealing the show. Everyone is impressed, including Benny, who is bursting with pride from head to toe as he plays.

The MUSIC continues playing over the next scene:

EXTERIOR PRAIRIE HOUSE—MORNING

Deadeye and Benny are mounted on their horses, waving goodbye to the prairie family. The Boy is wearing what used to be Benny's gun and holster set and cowboy hat.

The Prairie Man has his arm around Tessa's shoulder, as they and their kids watch Deadeye and Benny ride off across the prairie.

EXTERIOR RANGE LAND—DAY

A harmonica is playing "Red River Valley." Deadeye and Benny, on horseback, ride into the scene; and we see that it is Benny who is playing the harmonica.

Suddenly a shot rings out. Star rears. Deadeye spots a pickup truck barreling recklessly down a dirt road below.

DEADEYE

Runaway wagon! C'mon, Star!

Deadeye and Star race after the pickup truck.

The truck bounds down the road. Through the back of the cab window we see that the driver is a young woman (GIRL).

Deadeye catches up with the truck and jumps into
the back, on top of a pile of feed bags. Glancing
back through the cab window, the Girl spots
Deadeye and looks surprised. Deadeye maneuvers
to the top of the cab, then swings his feet in
through the open window on the driver's side.

100.

INTERIOR PICKUP CAB—DAY

The Girl is shocked to find Deadeye's boots in
her face; and she tries to push them back out the
window.

Deadeye works his legs in farther and farther,
though; and the truck starts swerving all over as
Deadeye's determined body begins forcing the Girl
over to the right side of the seat.

EXTERIOR PICKUP TRUCK—DAY

The truck is swerving all over the road.

INTERIOR PICKUP CAB—DAY

Finally, Deadeye's entire body drops inside the
cab.

                    DEADEYE

    Move over.

                     GIRL

    Hey, what the hell are you doing?

(STARTS PUNCHING DEADEYE)

    Get out of my truck, you dirty
    sonovabitch!

Deadeye and the Girl struggle for possession of
the wheel.

EXTERIOR PICKUP TRUCK—DAY

The truck swerves off the road and bounds down an
incline, headed directly for a huge rock. Just
before it almost slams into the rock, the truck
slides to a sudden stop.

INTERIOR PICKUP CAB—DAY

Deadeye is sitting at the wheel, his right foot still locked on the brake pedal. He and the Girl take a couple moments to catch their breath.

> GIRL
>
> Just what the hell do you think you're doing?

> DEADEYE
>
> Trying to save you, for crying out loud!

> GIRL
>
> Save me? Save me from what?

> DEADEYE
> (SURPRISED)
>
> From crashing!

> GIRL
>
> Crashing? I wasn't worried about crash-ing 'til you started climbing in the window and shoving me out of my truck!

EXTERIOR PICKUP TRUCK—DAY

Deadeye and the Girl climb out of the truck. The Girl is about 25, with a pretty, lightly-freckled face and long dark hair. She is wearing jeans and a light slipover top, with no bra, and sandals on her feet. Her dress and her demeanor reveal her to be at least slightly hip.

102.

                    DEADEYE
What about that shot I heard?

                     GIRL
Shot? (THINKS) You mean the backfire?
This truck always backfires!

(CHECKS DEADEYE'S GETUP)

What kind of trip are you on, anyway?

Benny rides up, flanked by Star.

                    DEADEYE
This here's my sidekick—Benny. He's an
Indian. And this is my horse, Star.
Oh yeah, and my name's Deadeye. I'm a
cowboy.

                     GIRL
Jeesuz, you are a screwball, aren't
you?

                    DEADEYE
Would you like me to drive your truck
back up to the road, Miss?

                     GIRL
(THOROUGHLY ANNOYED)
Listen, Deadhead...

                    DEADEYE
Deadeye.

                    GIRL

     Whatever your name is, get this and get
     it good: If you ever come near me or
     this truck again, you'll be lucky if
     you live to regret it! Now fuck off!

Girl hops in truck, revs up engine, and drives
back up towards the road.

                   DEADEYE

     Frisky little bobcat, ain't she?

EXTERIOR RANGE LAND—DAY

Deadeye and Benny, on horseback, ride to a crest
and then stop. Across the range they spot some
COWHANDS on horseback herding a group of about
ten cows.

                   DEADEYE

     Rustlers. Let's get 'em, Benny!

Deadeye draws his gun and lights out on Star.
He rides toward the Cowhands, firing his gun at
them, pulling trigger and making shooting noise.

     Ptew! Ptew! Ptew! Ptew!

Surprisingly, when the Cowhands see Deadeye
coming, they turn and ride off, leaving clouds of
dust in their wake.

When Deadeye arrives where the cows are, the
Cowhands have just disappeared over the ridge in
the distance.

Deadeye dismounts and begins checking the ground
for clues. Benny rides up.

Deadeye bends over and picks up something.

                    DEADEYE
        Look at this, Benny. (HOLDS UP A PIECE
        OF HORSESHOE) A broken horseshoe tip.
        It must've come from one of those rus-
        tlers' horses.

Deadeye examines it, then puts the horseshoe
piece in his pocket.

Suddenly, from another direction, come three

hard-riding COWHANDS, dressed in typical cowhand fashion and riding dark horses. They charge right up to Deadeye and Benny, and stop. One of them levels a rifle and cocks it.

                    RIFLEMAN
          Okay, you no good cattle thieves! This
          time we caught you red-handed!

106.

EXTERIOR RED RIVER—DAY

Deadeye and Benny, on horseback, flanked by the
Rifleman and the other two Cowhands, are riding
into the small town of Red River. They pass a
sign that says: WELCOME TO RED RIVER, LAST OF THE
OLD WEST.

The town has reminders of the modern era—automo-
biles, a Gulf Oil station, Coca Cola signs—but,
as in many such towns in 1977 Wyoming, there is
a definite effort to maintain the look of the
Old West—wide street, wooden sidewalks, Western-
style business signs, and even hitching posts for
horses.

The PEOPLE of Red River dress modern Western—
plenty of Stetson hats, leather vests and
high-heeled boots.

A large sign hanging across Main Street says: RED
RIVER WILD WEST DAYS CELEBRATION, and underneath:
JULY 14-24.

Deadeye's entourage stops directly in front of a
sign that says: SHERIFF'S OFFICE - JAIL.

INTERIOR RED RIVER JAIL—DAY

Deadeye and Benny are locked inside a jail cell.
(Deadeye is not wearing his play guns. They've
been confiscated by the Sheriff.)

                    BENNY

    Should we tell the Sheriff we wanna
    make a phone call?

                    DEADEYE

    I've got a better idea.

Deadeye moves to the barred window at the back of the cell and looks out into the open area behind the building. He WHISTLES loudly through the bars.

He waits, but nothing happens.

Deadeye WHISTLES again. He waits. Benny looks at Deadeye.

Just as Deadeye starts to whistle again, Star comes to the window.

DEADEYE

Good boy, Star!

EXTERIOR BACK OF JAIL BUILDING—DAY—MOMENTS LATER

Star is standing at the barred window. Deadeye, visible through the bars, has tied one end of a rope to the window bars and the other end to Star's saddle horn.

INTERIOR JAIL CELL—DAY

DEADEYE
(AT THE WINDOW)
Okay, Star. You know what to do.

EXTERIOR JAIL BUILDING—DAY

Star moves away from the window, as far as the rope will allow.

INTERIOR JAIL CELL—DAY

DEADEYE

Pull, Star. Pull!

108.

EXTERIOR JAIL BUILDING—DAY

Star pulls. But nothing happens.

INTERIOR JAIL CELL—DAY

                    DEADEYE
     C'mon, boy. You can do it!
     Pull! Pull!

EXTERIOR JAIL CELL—DAY

Star whinnies, digs his feet in and pulls hard.
But still no results.

INTERIOR JAIL CELL—DAY

                    DEADEYE
       Pull! Pull!

EXTERIOR JAIL CELL—DAY

Star struggles, rears and jumps, pulling with all
his might. Boom! The back wall of the jail comes
crashing down!

                    DEADEYE
       Yahoo!

Deadeye and Benny come running through the wall.
Deadeye unties the rope from Star's saddle horn
and mounts. Benny moves to the side of the building to get Lizard.

                    DEADEYE
       Head for the hills!

Deadeye, Star, Benny and Lizard take off towards open country.

The SHERIFF, a tall granite-jawed man, appears at the remains of the jail cell wall. He stares dumbfounded through the gigantic hole, watching Deadeye and Benny ride off.

EXTERIOR CAMPFIRE—NIGHT

Deadeye and Benny are camped for the night. Benny is sitting at the campfire, practicing some licks on his harmonica. Deadeye is pacing and thinking.

                              DEADEYE
        What would the Lone Ranger do in a case
        like this?

110.

                              BENNY
(BEAT)

        If he had any sense, man, he'd split.
        Look, Deadeye, why can't we just move
        on to some other town and have our
        first adventure there? Man, if that
        Sheriff in Red River catches us now,
        we'll be lucky to get outta jail in
        fifty years!

                             DEADEYE
(INTENSELY)

        Benny, there's somebody rustling cattle
        around here, and we're gonna find out
        who it is.

(STOPS AND THINKS)

        I've got it.

(CROUCHES DOWN NEXT TO BENNY)

        Now listen, Benny, here's the plan...

                                        DISSOLVE TO:

EXTERIOR RED RIVER—DAY

A bearded OLD PROSPECTOR hobbles down Main Street
and stops at a group of horses tied to a hitching
post. He begins lifting the horses' feet, one at
a time, checking the horseshoes.

The Prospector's fake beard comes loose at
the side; and as he pats it back in place, we
see that it is really Deadeye, disguised as a
prospector.

A figure wearing a large Indian headdress and
wrapped in a colorful Indian blanket approaches

from the opposite direction. We see that it is
Benny disguised as an old Indian.

As Benny approaches, Deadeye is holding a piece
of broken horseshoe in one hand, and lifting up a
horse's foot with the other.

                    BENNY

     Deadeye, this is ridiculous.

                    DEADEYE

     Did you check the horses at that end?

                    BENNY

     Yeah. No broken shoes. Look, man,
     this is hopeless. We ain't gonna find
     nothing here. Let's just forget those
     rustlers and get outta this town while
     we can.

Deadeye has checked all the horse hooves in the
group, to no avail. He stands in the hot sun,
momentarily stumped. Suddenly he looks up on the
wooden sidewalk and spots a BEARDED OLD MAN with
a frumpy hat. The Man is sitting in a chair,
leaning back against the building front. He sips
from a pint-sized bottle in a brown bag, then
places the bottle back inside his coat.

                    DEADEYE

(TO BENNY)

     Wait here.

Deadeye looks around, then walks over to the
Bearded Old Man, whom we will come to know as
SQUIRRELY.

112.

                    DEADEYE
(AFFECTING A VOICE TO FIT HIS DISGUISE)
     Hey, old timer—anybody ever tell you
     you look like Gabby Hayes?

                    SQUIRRELY

     Who?

                    DEADEYE

     Gabby Hayes. Anybody ever tell you you
     look like him?

                    SQUIRRELY

     Nope. Name's Elmo Scurly. Folks call me
     Squirrely.

                    DEADEYE

     Squirrely, huh? You, uh, you lived here
     all your life, Squirrely?

                    SQUIRRELY

     Not yet.

                    DEADEYE
(REACTS)
     Tell me, Squirrely, who's the boss of
     this town?

                    SQUIRRELY

     The boss?

                    DEADEYE
     Yeah, you know—the guy who owns everything.

                    SQUIRRELY

     Oh, I guess you mean Scotty
     MacPheeters. He owns all the land.
     Lives on a ranch a few miles outside of
     town.

EXTERIOR MacPHEETERS RANCH—DAY

Deadeye and Benny are sneaking around behind the
MacPheeters ranch house. Benny follows Deadeye
to a couple horses tied outside the stable, and
watches as Deadeye begins picking up the horses'
feet and checking the horseshoes.

                     BENNY

     What makes you think we're gonna find
     anything here?

                    DEADEYE

     Trust me.

SFX: A rifle is cocked O.S.

Deadeye and Benny turn around. Staring at them is
the Girl they met in the "runaway" pickup truck.
(We will come to know her as RAINEY.) Standing
next to her, holding a rifle on Deadeye and
Benny, is the Rifleman who escorted them to the
Red River jail.

                    DEADEYE

(REFERRING TO RAINEY)

     Well, what do you know. It's the Bobcat.

114.

RIFLEMAN

(TO RAINEY)

These are the two rustlers we caught in
the North Pasture, Miss MacPheeters.

RAINEY

Well, now, I'll bet my father would
like to meet you two.

INTERIOR MacPHEETERS RANCH HOUSE—DAY

Mr. Alistair "Scotty" MacPheeters, an aging man
in his late 60s, is talking into a wall phone in
a small room just off his living room.

MacPHEETERS

(ON PHONE)

Okay, Sheriff. Right. Bye.

MacPheeters, carrying a shillelagh and walking
with a limp, moves into the living room and sits
on a chair across from Deadeye and Benny, who
are seated on the couch. Rainey is sitting on
the edge of a nearby desk; and the Rifleman, his
rifle resting across his chest, is standing guard
at the front door.

MacPHEETERS

(TO DEADEYE)

So you say you don't know anything
about who's been stealin' my cattle?

                    DEADEYE

     That's right, Mr. MacPheeters. But
     Benny and I are going to find out. At
     first we thought you might have some-
     thing to do with the rustling. That was
     before we knew it was your cattle, of
     course.

MacPheeters and Rainey exchange amused glances.

                    MacPHEETERS

     I believe you. You boys don't look
     like rustlers to me. What do you think,
     Rainey?

                    RAINEY

     I guess you're right, Dad. I don't
     think these two could ride herd if they
     had to.

                    MacPHEETERS

     I just talked to the Sheriff, and he
     agreed to let you go as long as I'm
     not gonna press charges. But he did say
     there was one condition.

EXTERIOR RED RIVER—DAY

Establishing shot of Red River.

EXTERIOR BACK OF JAIL BUILDING—DAY

Deadeye and Benny are repairing the hole in the
back of the Red River jail wall. They are sweating
profusely in the hot sun, struggling to fit the
dusty bricks in place and seal them with cement.

116.

SFX (O.S.): A gunshot.

Deadeye and Benny continue working without
looking up.

SFX (O.S.): Two more gunshots

Pull back to show the Sheriff a few yards away.
He is getting some target practice, shooting at
cans he has set up on a log in the open area
behind the jail. Sheriff WALT CARTER is a tall,
stocky, square-jawed man pushing 50. He has the
confident air of a man who may once have been
a true Western hero, but has now opted for the
peace and tranquility of Red River.

Having missed one of the cans, the Sheriff takes
careful aim again, using both hands to steady his
gun, and fires. The can jumps.

Deadeye has stopped work momentarily, and is
looking towards the Sheriff. Deadeye wipes his
brow and sits on a pile of bricks.

                    DEADEYE
(CALLS)
        You're a good shot, Sheriff.

                    SHERIFF
        Ah, I'm rusty. Only practice like this
        once a year. Gotta get ready for Wild
        West Days.

Begins reloading his gun.

        Most times Red River's a real peaceable
        town. Quiet. No trouble. Only time I've
        gotta earn my money is during Wild West

Days. That's why I hate July. Usually
it's strangers that cause the trouble.
They come into town to celebrate, get
boozed up, and start thinking they're
really living back in the Old West.
Happens every year.

Deadeye takes a silver dollar from his pocket,
looks at it, and flips it in the air.

DEADEYE

Sheriff, did you ever throw up a silver
dollar and shoot a hole in it?

SHERIFF
(SMILES)

You kidding? I've seen a lot of fancy
shooting in my time. Ain't never seen
anybody who could do that, though. That
stuff only happens in the movies.

DEADEYE

Tell you what, Sheriff. I'll bet you
I can toss this silver dollar up and
shoot a hole in it dead center.

The Sheriff looks at Deadeye to see if he's
serious. Benny looks at Deadeye to see if he's
serious.

SHERIFF
(DISBELIEVING)

Sure you can.

                         DEADEYE
          I'll make a deal with you, Sheriff. If
          I do it, you finish repairing this wall
          yourself. If I miss, Benny and I will
          not only finish this wall, but we'll be
          your slaves for the rest of the week,
          doing anything you need done around the
          jail.

                          BENNY
     (ASIDE, FLABBERGASTED)
          Deadeye, what the...

                         DEADEYE
     (ASIDE)
          Trust me, Benny.

                         SHERIFF
     (SMILING)
          Okay, you've got a deal.

Deadeye moves to Sheriff. Sheriff hands Deadeye
the gun.

          One shot, right?

Deadeye looks at the gun, twirls it in his hand
to get the feel. He licks the tenseness from his
lips, takes a deep breath and concentrates.

The Sheriff and Benny look on, anxious.

Deadeye puts the gun through the front of his
belt. He tosses the silver dollar, pulls the gun
and shoots—all in one swift, impressive motion.

They all move to the silver dollar. Deadeye takes
it from the ground and holds it up. There is a
bullet hole dead center!

The Sheriff's jaw drops and Benny's eyes pop out.
Benny and the Sheriff both look at Deadeye in
utter disbelief.

                    DEADEYE
     Why do you think they call me
     "Deadeye"?

EXTERIOR JAIL BUILDING—DAY

FLIP TO:

The Sheriff, sleeves rolled up and face sweating,
is fixing the jail wall himself. He hurls a brick
at the ground in disgust.

EXTERIOR RED RIVER—DAY

High, panning shot of Main Street. Stop in front
of the store window that says: LANGFORD WESTERN
CLOTHING.

Deadeye exits from the clothing store, impressively dressed in a new cowboy outfit. He is
wearing everything but guns. This time he really
looks the role. Tom Mix or Roy Rogers never
looked more convincing.

Deadeye turns on the wooden sidewalk and checks
his image in the store window. He studies a
poster sign in the window that says: CROSS
COUNTRY HORSE RACE, July 16, 10:00 a.m. Start At
West End Of Town, WIN A NEW SADDLE, Sponsored By
The Red River Wild West Days Committee.

Deadeye looks in the store window again,
straightening his handsome new six-gallon hat.
In the window he sees the reflection of Rainey
MacPheeters, loading her pickup truck across the
street in front of the RED RIVER GENERAL STORE.

120.

Deadeye turns and heads across the street.

Rainey is loading some large bags of cattle feed onto her pickup truck. Deadeye approaches.

                         DEADEYE
(TIPPING HIS HAT)
     Howdy, Miss.

He lifts a bag of feed and starts to put it on the truck.

                         RAINEY
     Look, Sir Galahad, if I want any help
     from you I'll ask for it, okay?

                         DEADEYE
(SHRUGS)
     Suit yourself, Bobcat.

Deadeye tosses the bag of feed to Rainey and it knocks her down, breaking in the process and spilling feed all over her.

Rainey is fit to be tied; but she grits her teeth and doesn't say a word.

Deadeye moves to the sidewalk in front of the General Store.

Rainey climbs into her pickup truck, slams the door, and tries to start the engine. But the truck won't start. She tries again and again, but no luck.

                         RAINEY
     Shit!

DEADEYE

Get a horse.

Rainey throws him a pissed-off look and climbs
out of the truck.

Tell you what, Bobcat. Let's get this
truck of yours towed to a garage, and
I'll give you a ride home on Star.

RAINEY

Thanks, but I'd rather crawl.

EXTERIOR OPEN ROAD—DAY

Rainey is walking barefoot alongside the empty
road, holding a sandal in each hand. Deadeye,
mounted on Star, is riding a few feet behind
Rainey, playing his guitar (not that well) and
singing "Red River Valley."

RAINEY
(MAD)

Why are you following me?

DEADEYE
(SNIFFING)

You smell like a walking bag of cattle
feed?

RAINEY

That's your fault.

                    DEADEYE

That's why I'm following you. I'd feel
bad if you got stampeded by a herd of
hungry cows.

Rainey can't help smiling.

                    RAINEY

Who are you, anyway?

                    DEADEYE

I'm a cowboy.

                    RAINEY

I mean, what do you do? Why did you
come to Red River?

                    DEADEYE

I came here to find out who's rustling
your father's cattle.

Rainey smiles, and searches Deadeye's face for
another answer.

How long's the rustling been going on?

                    RAINEY

Aw, we've always had trouble with
rustlers. Seems to be getting worse
lately, though. Maybe it's the beef
shortage.

                    DEADEYE

Do you work on the ranch full time?

124.

                    RAINEY

    Just in the summer. The rest of the
    year I teach college in Laramie.

(WINCES AS SHE STEPS ON A STONE)

    Since my mother died, I've been coming
    home whenever I can to help Dad. Fact
    is, he's getting too old to run the
    place by himself. I keep telling him to
    sell it, but he's stubborn.

                    DEADEYE

    A teacher, huh? What do you teach?

                    RAINEY

    History.

                    DEADEYE

    A history major.

                    RAINEY

    Actually, I majored in Political
    Science. When I was young and foolish,
    I wanted to go into politics. I pic-
    tured myself running for office and
    changing the world.

                    DEADEYE

    What changed your mind?

                    RAINEY

    I don't know. A lot of things, I guess.

Beat. Another angle.

                        DEADEYE

    I noticed that sign in town about the
    cross country horse race. Are you plan-
    ning to enter?

                        RAINEY

    No. Are you?

                        DEADEYE
(SMILING AS HE CHECKS STAR'S SADDLE)

    Yeah, I think I will. Star could use a
    new saddle.

                        RAINEY
(SMIRKING AT DEADEYE'S COCKINESS)

    What makes you think you've got a
    chance?

                        DEADEYE

    What makes you think I don't?

                        RAINEY

    El Diablo.

                        DEADEYE

    Who?

                        RAINEY

    El Diablo—the fastest horse in the
    county. He's a thoroughbred.

                    DEADEYE

     Well, if you're betting any money, bet
     it on Star.

(PATS HIS HORSE)

     Star and I are gonna beat 'em all.
     Right, boy?

Star whinnies and shakes his head up, then
down. Rainey looks surprised at first—it almost
seemed as if Star actually shook his head 'Yes'
in answer to Deadeye. Rainey quickly realizes, though, that it must have been just a
coincidence.

                    DEADEYE

     Tell you what: I'll give you one more
     chance. How'd you like to take a ride
     on the best horse in Wyoming?

Rainey stops and looks up at Deadeye, softening.

                    RAINEY

     Well, these stones aren't getting any
     softer on my feet.

Rainey smiles and moves to Deadeye. He puts his
guitar aside and helps Rainey to swing up onto
Star, behind the saddle.

                    RAINEY

     C'mon, cowboy, I'll take you someplace
     special.

Long shot: They gallop off down the road.

DISSOLVE through a SERIES OF SHOTS with Deadeye and Rainey riding along narrow paths in
the woods.

                    DEADEYE
     Where are we going?

                    RAINEY
     I hope it's still there. I haven't been
     there in years.

DISSOLVE to Deadeye and Rainey riding alongside a
clear stream which leads to a picture book pond
in the middle of the woods.

     Here it is. The old swimming hole.

EXTERIOR SWIMMING HOLE—DAY

Deadeye and Rainey are standing at the swimming
hole, staring at their reflections in the water.
Deadeye is awed at the natural beauty and tranquility of the scene.

                    RAINEY
     I'm gonna get rid of this feed smell.

She strips off her clothes—to Deadeye's shocked
surprise—and runs into the water. Deadeye watches
Rainey's soft, nude body move through the water
like a mermaid.

                    RAINEY
(CALLING FROM WATER)
     Come on in!

                    DEADEYE
(NERVOUSLY FUMBLING WITH HIS HAT)
     Uh, no thanks. I'll just watch. I mean,
     I uh, I forgot my trunks.

Rainey smiles.

EXTERIOR WOODS—DAY

Deadeye and Rainey—her hair still wet from her
swim—are riding through the woods on Star. Birds
chirp; a slight breeze blows; and the clean,
natural beauty of the scene is striking. Deadeye
notices some flowers—blue petals with yellow
"eyes"—growing along the trail.

                    DEADEYE
     Look at those blue flowers.

                    RAINEY
(LOOKS)
     Those are wild forget-me-nots. Pretty,
     aren't they?

                    DEADEYE
     So that's what forget-me-nots look
     like, huh?

                    RAINEY
     They used to grow everywhere around
     here. When I was a kid, we'd even find
     'em growing up through the wooden side-
     walks in town.

Star stops and Rainey dismounts to pick some
forget-me-nots. She hands one to Deadeye, keeps

a small bouquet for herself, and, with Deadeye's help, climbs back onto Star.

They ride along, smiling, as the sun begins to set.

EXTERIOR RED RIVER—DAY

Deadeye and Benny are walking along Main Street. The town is booming with the anticipated excitement of Wild West Days. Colorful shirts and old-style cowboy outfits abound. Many women are wearing long prairie gowns.

130.

A small BOY, sporting a hat almost as tall as he
is, is twirling a rope and trying to lasso a post
outside the General Store.

Deadeye and Benny approach the boy. Deadeye stops.

                    DEADEYE
          Here, pardner, let me show you how to
          do that.

The boy hands Deadeye the rope.

Deadeye lengthens the loop and starts twirling it
over his head. Benny's face anticipates disaster.

          Keep it over your head like this, see;
          and then when you toss it, follow
          through.

Deadeye lets go of the loop and, to Benny's
surprise, lassos the post perfectly. The boy,
anxious to try Deadeye's advice, takes the rope
back from Deadeye; and Deadeye and Benny move on.

                    BENNY
          Where did you learn how to do that?

                    DEADEYE
          All cowboys know how to throw a lariat.

Deadeye and Benny move to the SILVER DOLLAR
SALOON, Red River's genuine Western-style hangout
on Main Street.

INTERIOR SILVER DOLLAR SALOON—DAY

The Silver Dollar Saloon is preserved in true
Western decor, with swinging double doors, round
wood tables, stand-up bar, etc. The saloon is

peppered with PATRONS—most drinking, and all touched with the excitement of Wild West Days.

Deadeye and Benny enter through the swinging doors and approach the bar. The BARTENDER, a middle-aged man, moves to Deadeye.

                    DEADEYE
(TO BARTENDER)
     Give me a glass of milk.

Bartender looks to Benny. Benny hesitates, then orders.

                    BENNY
     Make that two.

As Deadeye and Benny wait for their drinks, they notice a group of rowdy young COWHANDS at the other end of the bar. The Cowhands have grabbed an old man's hat and are playing keep-away with it, teasing the old man as he tries to retrieve it. The old man is Squirrely.

An athletic-looking cowhand with prominent jowls—nicknamed BULLDOG—holds Squirrely's hat out to him; but as Squirrely reaches for it, Bulldog gleefully tosses it to another Cowhand.

                    SQUIRRELY
     C'mon, punks. Give it.

                    BULLDOG
(MOCKING)
     'Punks'? Oooh, Squirrely's getting mad!
The other Cowhands laugh.

132.

                    BARTENDER
(AS HE GETS DEADEYE'S AND BENNY'S DRINKS)
    Give him his hat, Bulldog.

                    BULLDOG
    You want your hat, Squirrely? We'll
    give you your hat. But you gotta do a
    dance for us first, okay? Right, Spike?

A lanky cowhand called SPIKE laughs uproariously
at the thought.

                     SPIKE
    Right! Make him dance, Bulldog—just
    like in the cowboy movies!

Squirrely's hat has been tossed back to Bulldog.

                    BULLDOG
(LAUGHING, TO BARTENDER)
    Lemme borrow that piece of yours, Duke.

Bulldog hoists himself over the bar, leans down,
reaches under the bar and comes up with the
Bartender's gun.

                    BARTENDER
    Bulldog...

                    BULLDOG
    C'mon, Squirrely. Dance!

Laughing, Bulldog aims the gun at the floor and
fires a shot near Squirrely's feet. To save his
toes, a frightened Squirrely attempts to dance as
the Cowhands all go crazy with laughter.

At the sound of the gunshot, everyone in the saloon stops and turns his attention to the circle of Cowhands around Squirrely. Deadeye quickly moves to the Cowhands.

                    DEADEYE
     Okay, that's enough.

The Cowhands stop and look at Deadeye.

(TO BULLDOG)
     Let him alone.

All are surprised at Deadeye's command.

                    BULLDOG
     Well, now, who is this brave dude?

                    DEADEYE
     My name's Deadeye.

                    BULLDOG
     Deadeye? (LAUGHS) Say, ain't you the
     dude they say can shoot a hole in a
     silver dollar?

(CHECKS HIM OVER)
     Well, now, anybody who can shoot like
     that must be a hell of a dancer, too.
     Don't you think, boys?

The Cowhands chuckle, and a couple say:

     "Right, Bulldog!"

SPIKE

Hey, Bulldog, see if he can do the
mashed potatoes.

The Cowhands all laugh. Bulldog throws
Squirrely's hat to Squirrely.

BARTENDER

(FROM BEHIND BAR)

C'mon, Bulldog. Knock it off and give
me my gun back.

BULLDOG

    In a minute, Duke.

(MOTIONS WITH GUN)

    Step aside, boys. Give Deadeye here
    some room to trot.

(AIMS GUN AT DEADEYE'S FEET)

    Okay, feets, do your stuff.

Deadeye swiftly kicks the gun from Bulldog's
hand, then throws a hard right to Bulldog's jaw,
sending him sprawling to the ground.

136.

Deadeye picks up the gun and points it at
Bulldog.

                         DEADEYE
     Okay, get up.

He does.

          Let's see how well you can dance.

Deadeye grabs Spike and shoves him toward
Bulldog.

                         DEADEYE
(TO SPIKE)
          You too, pardner. Let's see if you can
          do the mashed potatoes.

Some of the bystanders chuckle.

          Dance!

Deadeye aims the gun at their feet and Bulldog
and Spike start dancing immediately.
The crowd roars with laughter.

          I think they could use a little music
          to help 'em keep in step, Benny.

Benny takes out his harmonica and starts blowing
"Turkey in the Straw" while Bulldog and Spike
dance.

                         BULLDOG
(ANGRY AND EMBARRASSED)
          You're gonna pay for this, Deadeye.

The Sheriff enters the saloon.

                    SHERIFF

     All right, boys, what's going on here?

Benny stops playing. Sheriff looks at Deadeye.

                    DEADEYE

     Bulldog here was just showing us a
     dance, Sheriff.

The Sheriff moves to Deadeye and takes the gun.

                    BARTENDER

     That's my gun, Sheriff.

                    SHERIFF
(CHECKS GUN AND THEN PLACES IT ON THE BAR)
     Try to hang on to it, huh, Duke?

(TO THE CROWD)
     Okay, break it up. Everybody.

The crowd scatters. Bulldog picks up his hat,
slaps it against his leg and throws Deadeye a
dirty look as he moves off with Spike.

                    SHERIFF
(TO DEADEYE)
     I don't know who started this, Deadeye,
     but I'll give you some advice. People
     around here don't like strangers stick-
     ing their nose where it don't belong.
     If I was you, I'd get outta Red River
     before you find yourself in some real
     trouble.

138.

The Sheriff moves off and Deadeye and Benny
move to the bar. Squirrely, holding his hat,
approaches Deadeye.

                    SQUIRRELY
          Thanks for what you done there, sonny.

                    DEADEYE
          It was a pleasure.

                    SQUIRRELY
          My name is Elmo Scurly. They call me
          Squirrely.

                    DEADEYE
          Yeah, I know. My name's Deadeye.
          And this is my sidekick, Benny. He's an
          Indian.

                    BENNY
          I wish you'd quit telling everybody I'm
          an Indian, Deadeye. I...

                    SQUIRRELY
          I knowed you was an Injun right off. I
          can always tell an Injun.

(BENNY REACTS)
          Nice to know you.

(TO DEADEYE)
          You two make a great team.

Deadeye smiles proudly.

EXTERIOR RED RIVER—DAY

In tight on huge banner that says: CROSS COUNTRY HORSE RACE. Pull back to show a group of horses being walked and rubbed down by their RIDERS, in preparation for the big race. The town is bustling with PEOPLE waiting for the start of the race, which will signal the official beginning of Red River's Wild West Days celebration.

Nearby, at the edge of town, a row of booths has been constructed where Crow and Sioux INDIANS from the Reservations have come to display and sell their handcrafted wares. Benny moves along the row of booths, looking at the variety of items. He stops at one booth and stares at the beaded headbands on display there. An old SQUAW in the booth watches as Benny picks up one of the headbands and examines it. He holds the headband, admiring its expert beadwork and colorful design. He sees the Squaw watching him, smiles, puts the headband back, and moves on.

Deadeye is tightening Star's saddle, preparing for the race. Rainey spots Deadeye and Star, and approaches.

                    RAINEY
     You're really gonna race, huh, cowboy?

                    DEADEYE
     I told you I was. I'm gonna win, too.

                    RAINEY
     Think your horse can beat that black
     stallion?

(NODS)

140.

Focus on a beautiful black horse who is mounted
by Bulldog. At the horse's side are his owner
(GORDON BRAXTON, a man of about forty-five who
is wearing a fancy black hat, a well-tailored
Western suit, and sports a neatly-trimmed moustache) and some interested COWHANDS.

                    DEADEYE

        Is that, uh...

                    RAINEY

        El Diablo? Yeah. Pretty horse, isn't
        he?

                    DEADEYE
(PATS STAR CONFIDENTLY)

        Not as pretty as Star.

                    RAINEY

        Gordon Braxton, the man with the fancy
        suit, owns him. Bulldog Meachum is
        riding him.

Deadeye stares at Bulldog and their eyes meet.

                    DEADEYE

        Yeah. Bulldog and I met before.

              LOUDSPEAKER (MALE V.O.)

        Ladies and gentlemen, the Red River
        Cross Country Horse Race is about to
        commence. Riders to your mounts.

Two MEN, one at each end, are holding a long rope
stretched to mark the starting line for the race.

About twenty-five Riders walk their horses into place behind the rope. The Riders remain on the ground alongside their horses, holding the reins. Deadeye is stationed about five horses down from Bulldog.

The CROWD gathers in anticipation. Squirrely crosses to Benny, who is watching from the sidelines.

                    SQUIRRELY
     Guess you're rooting for Deadeye, ain't ya?

                    BENNY
     Yeah.

                    SQUIRRELY
     So am I. Figure that thoroughbred El
     Diablo's gonna win, though. But I
     always like to root for the underdog.

(BENNY STARES OUT AT THE FIELD OF HORSES AS SQUIRRELY LOOKS AT THE SCAR ON BENNY'S NECK)

     Say, how'd you get that nasty rope burn
     on your neck? Somebody try to hang you?

Benny forces a smile and lowers his chin as Rainey approaches.

Deadeye, standing alongside Star, spots Benny, Squirrely and Rainey on the sidelines. Benny and Squirrely wave "Good Luck" to Deadeye. He waves back, and tips his hat to Rainey.

Some PEOPLE are gathered atop a platform. Among them is a MAN at the loudspeaker.

Angle: Riders standing next to their horses, looking up to the platform.

                    MAN (ON LOUDSPEAKER)

      You all know the rules. The course is
      staked out across the range and fin-
      ishes back here where you started. Do
      not mount until you hear the sound of
      the gun.

The Riders stand anxiously by their horses.
Deadeye glances at Bulldog. Bulldog looks at
Deadeye and smirks.

LOUDSPEAKER (V.O.)

Riders to your mark... (THE ROPE IS
DROPPED) Get set... (A GUN IS FIRED)

The Crowd cheers. Riders scramble onto their
horses and head out across the range. One
horse is spooked by the gun shot and takes off
in another direction, with the would-be Rider
chasing after him.

Deadeye and Star get off to a good start. So does
Bulldog, who soon moves into the lead.

144.

HORSE RACE—DAY

Horses' hooves pound furiously across the range. Deadeye and Star are pacing themselves well, running about fifth. At one point, the horses reach a creek and have to jump across. One horse falls, and the Rider ends up in the creek. Another horse, one of the leaders, trips in a gopher hole and his Rider flies off.

As they round a tall flag marker, Deadeye and Star start to make their move. With Deadeye voicing encouragement, Star passes two horses, and moves into second place behind Bulldog and El Diablo.

El Diablo and Star race neck and neck across the range, leaving all other contenders behind.

Using the reins, Bulldog whips El Diablo furiously.

Riding side by side, Bulldog and Deadeye begin bumping slightly. Finally, Bulldog reaches over and tries to shove Deadeye off Star. Deadeye stays upright, and Bulldog tries again. Bulldog manages to knock Deadeye off balance, but Deadeye grabs Bulldog and they both go tumbling to the ground.

Bulldog jumps up first and runs to the horses; but before mounting, he takes out a pocket knife and cuts Star's saddle cinches. Bulldog hops on El Diablo and rides off.

Deadeye gets up, jumps on Star; and as Star takes off, the saddle and Deadeye slide to the ground. Deadeye bounces back up, runs and springs onto Star from behind—Red Ryder style. Now minus a saddle, Deadeye and Star light out after Bulldog.

Bulldog continues to whip El Diablo while Deadeye
and Star gain ground. The town appears in the
distance, and PEOPLE begin to scream and cheer.

Deadeye and Bulldog are racing neck and neck.
El Diablo is starting to tire, and Bulldog is
cussing him and whipping. But Star sees nothing
but the finish line. Riding bareback, Deadeye is
holding on for his life as Star begins to pass El
Diablo.

The Crowd is going wild. Gordon Braxton, El
Diablo's owner, is shocked to see his horse
behind. Benny, Squirrely and Rainey are shocked

to see Deadeye leading. The three of them get completely caught up in the excitement and begin cheering wildly for Deadeye.

Crossing the finish line, Deadeye and Star beat a tired El Diablo by a full two lengths. Benny, Squirrely and Rainey lead the Crowd of con-gratulators. Deadeye dismounts in front of the platform and hugs Star. An OFFICIAL takes first prize, a fancy new silver-studded saddle, and lifts it onto Star's back. The Man at the loud-speaker takes some written information from the WOMAN next to him and announces the results as Deadeye and Star are being congratulated.

                    LOUDSPEAKER (V.O.)
          Ladies and gentlemen, the winner of
          this year's Cross Country Horse Race
          is Star, ridden by Deadeye. Finishing
          second is El Diablo, ridden by Bulldog
          Meachum. And in third place, Black
          Lightning, ridden by Chester Fox. The
          grand prize, a new silver-studded
          saddle, goes to Deadeye and Star.

Deadeye tightens the saddle on Star and pats him.

                    DEADEYE
          There, Star, how do you like that?

(ADMIRING THE SADDLE ON STAR)
          You're the prettiest horse there ever was.

Star whinnies. Deadeye mounts and pats Star. A PHOTOGRAPHER with a large Polaroid camera moves in to take pictures of the winning horse and rider. Deadeye gets Star to rear, standing up straight, as the Photographer snaps the shot. FREEZE FRAME: This pose is one that would make even Roy Rogers and Trigger envious. We see Deadeye as an impressive, authentic-looking cowboy hero, mounted on Star, his strikingly beautiful white horse, sporting a brand new saddle.

MUSIC (VOICE OVER):

DEADEYE IS STRUMMING GUITAR AND SINGING "RED RIVER VALLEY." CARRY TO NEXT SCENE.

DEADEYE (VOICE OVER)

From this valley they say you are going. We will miss your bright eyes and sweet smile...

INTERIOR MacPHEETERS RANCH HOUSE—NIGHT

As singing continues, pull back from photo of Deadeye and Star, which is now mounted in a frame on a table behind the sofa in the living room of the MacPheeters ranch house.

Deadeye and Rainey are sitting on the sofa. Deadeye is playing his guitar and singing. His singing isn't bad, but his playing isn't good. Rainey gets up, disappears for a moment, then returns with a container similar to a coffee can. Listening politely while Deadeye continues to play and sing, Rainey opens the container and starts to roll a joint.

Deadeye's eyes reflect his shocked surprise. Half pretending not to notice what Rainey is doing, Deadeye continues playing and singing, trying to cover the chord and verse mistakes he starts making. Rainey gets the number rolled, lights up, and takes a long drag.

148.

Deadeye can't ignore it any longer. He completes
the chorus to "Red River Valley," then stops.
Rainey passes the joint to Deadeye, but Deadeye
doesn't take it.

                    RAINEY

          Come on. Take a hit. It's the best
          stuff around. Mountain grown.

                    DEADEYE

          I didn't know you smoked.

                    RAINEY

          What are you looking at me like that
          for? (JOKING) You're not a narc, are
          you?

Deadeye doesn't smile or answer. A silent pause,
as Rainey pales.

          Are you?

                    DEADEYE

          No, I'm not a narc.

                    RAINEY
        (RELIEVED)
          Hey, don't do that. You scared the shit
          out of me, you know that?

                    DEADEYE

          That's another thing. You shouldn't
          cuss like that.

                    RAINEY

          Huh?

                    DEADEYE

          You shouldn't use those words.

                    RAINEY
          (SMILING)
               Are you serious? You mean you never say
               "shit"?

                    DEADEYE

          Not any more.

                    RAINEY

               Well maybe you should. A psychol-
               ogy teacher friend of mine says that
               cussing relieves your frustrations.
               People who cuss live longer.

Rainey takes another deep drag on the joint and
holds it out to Deadeye. Deadeye shakes his
head. Rainey sets the joint on an ashtray. She's
getting high.

                    RAINEY

               Come on, let me hear you say "Shit."

Deadeye won't.

               Maybe it'll relieve some of your
               tension. Loosen you up a bit.

Rainey leans against Deadeye and tries to form
the word with his mouth.

150.

                    RAINEY (CONT'D)
          Sh-i-t. Try it. Just put your lips like
          this and say sh-it.

          Sh-it. Shit. Say sh—like in shucks. Then
          it. Shit.

Rainey laughs. Deadeye, not sure what to do,
starts to reach for his guitar. Rainey cuts him
off.

                    RAINEY
          I know what we need—music.

(GETS UP AND MOVES TO STEREO, TAKES SOME RECORDS
FROM THE RACK BELOW)

          Do you like the Stones?

(SPOTS A RECORD)

          Oh, here's my favorite.

(PUTS RECORD ON)

Rainey goes back to the sofa. As the Rolling
Stones sing "Monkey Man," Rainey slides next to
Deadeye and tries to seduce him. She takes his
hat off and rubs her fingers through his hair.
She puts her arm around him. She pecks at his
neck, then kisses him full on the mouth.

Deadeye pulls away.

                    RAINEY
          What's the matter?

                    DEADEYE
You put your tongue in my mouth.

                    RAINEY
(OFFENDED)
     Gee, I'm sorry!

                   DEADEYE
     No, it's...it's nothing against you.
     It's just... Well, you know, what would
     my fans think?

Rainey studies his face.

     I mean, what would you think if you
     saw Dale Evans stick her tongue in Roy
     Rogers' mouth?

                    RAINEY
     You're really serious, aren't you?
     You're really fucking serious.

(BEAT)

     Listen, Deadeye, I like you. But you're
     carrying this game too far. This stuff
     about Benny being your Indian sidekick,
     and you being a cowboy... Shit, Benny's
     no more an Indian than I am. And you're
     no more a cowboy than I am. You've
     gotta grow up, Deadeye. Get a hold on
     reality. You're not Roy Rogers; and
     life isn't a fucking cowboy movie.

Deadeye reflects, then slowly picks up his hat and
guitar and moves toward the door in silence. Rainey
is upset, sad that she had to say what she said.

EXTERIOR MacPHEETERS RANCH HOUSE—NIGHT

152.

Deadeye comes through the front door and closes
it behind him. He moves down the porch steps
and over to where Star is hitched to a post. He
straps the guitar over his shoulder and takes
Star's reins. He stares into Star's eyes and pats
his horse's neck.

                    DEADEYE
(QUIETLY)
        You know, Star, the hardest thing in
        the world is believing in yourself when
        nobody else does.

Deadeye mounts Star and, as they ride slowly
away, the Rolling Stones sing loudly from the
stereo in the MacPheeters house.

                              DISSOLVE TO:

EXTERIOR RED RIVER—DAY

Deadeye rides into town on Star. He stops in
front of a hitching post, dismounts, and proceeds
to loop Star's reins around the post. He glances
down at the ground and there in the dust, right
beside him, is a horseshoe print showing a broken
shoe.

Deadeye picks up the hind leg of the big brown
horse next to him and sees that the horse does
indeed have a broken shoe. Deadeye quickly takes
the piece of broken shoe from his pocket and,
sure enough, it matches exactly.

Deadeye moves out of sight into a nearby alley to
wait for the horse's owner to appear. From across
the street, through an office door that says
THE BRAXTON INVESTMENT CO., INC., comes Bulldog,
Spike and another Cowhand we've seen with them

before. They all walk straight to their horses—
Spike's is the one with the broken shoe.

                    DEADEYE
(TO HIMSELF)

    Now we're getting somewhere!

They look around; Bulldog and Spike shove pack-
ages into their saddlebags; and the three of them
mount and ride off.

Deadeye crosses the street and sneaks around
behind the office of THE BRAXTON INVESTMENT CO.,
INC. Just as he is about to boost himself up
to a window and look inside, Deadeye is hit on
the head from behind and knocked to the ground,
unconscious. Next to Deadeye's body stand two
feet—both wearing black WING TIP SHOES. A medium
shot shows a middle-aged MAN in a city suit and
black wing tips standing over Deadeye.

EXTERIOR HIGHWAY—DAY

A station wagon—the same one we've seen earlier—
is driving along an open highway. At first we
see only the side of this shiny, mechanical
vehicle as it speeds along, contrasting with the
natural scenery in the background. As the car
pulls straightaway, we move in tight on the rear
license plate. It is a MINNESOTA plate.

                              DISSOLVE TO:

EXTERIOR ANOTHER HIGHWAY—NIGHT

The same station wagon is rolling along.

                              DISSOLVE TO:

154.

EXTERIOR MINNEAPOLIS—DAY

High, establishing shot of Minneapolis. Pick up the station wagon on the freeway below.

EXTERIOR HOSPITAL—DAY

Exterior shot of a large hospital. In tight on sign that says:

CLAREMONT STATE HOSPITAL.

INTERIOR HOSPITAL CORRIDOR—DAY

Three men are walking down the corridor. Two are dressed in white uniforms, and the other is wearing a suit. The man in the suit is Norbert L. Mechley, psychiatrist. The other two are DR. FOSTER—a medical doctor—and his INTERN. Mechley is looking at a clipboard as they walk.

> DR. FOSTER
>
> He's been raising hell all weekend. He still insists he's a cowboy.

They stop in front of door #507. Mechley hands the clipboard to Dr. Foster. Foster peeks through the door's small window and sees Deadeye across the room, reclining on the room's only bed.

INTERIOR HOSPITAL ROOM—DAY

Deadeye is still dressed in his cowboy outfit. The door opens and Mechley walks in. In addition to the bed, the room is furnished with two chairs and a night stand.

> MECHLEY
>
> Hi, Richard.

The door closes behind him.

                    DEADEYE
Well, well... Mechley, I should've
known she'd be sending you here. Now
I can add you to my list. Let's see:
there's Peggy; that detective she hired
to find me; the hospital staff; and
now you. I'm gonna sue all of you for
everything you've got!

                    MECHLEY
Richard, we want to help you. You have
a problem.

                    DEADEYE
My sister is the one with the problem.
I hope for her sake she can find a good
lawyer.

                    MECHLEY
Richard, Peggy's worried sick about
you. She's afraid you're going to
end up like your Uncle Buford. You're
exhibiting all the same symptoms.

Deadeye frowns and reflects.

     Richard, you've...

                    DEADEYE
My name is Deadeye. I'm a cowboy.

                    MECHLEY
(SOFTLY AND DIRECTLY)
     Richard, you are not a cowboy.

(BEAT)

     Your name is Richard Wentworth, and
     you're a lawyer.

                    DEADEYE
(THINKS)
     I'm no lawyer. That was somebody else's
     idea. My whole life's been somebody
     else's idea. But I'm changing that now.
     From now on, I'm living my life the way
     I wanna live it. (EMPHATIC) I'm through
     compromising.

                    MECHLEY
     Richard, life is a compromise.

                    DEADEYE
     Maybe for you it is; but not for me.

(SMILES PROUDLY)

     I'm a hero now, Mechley. A cowboy hero.
     And heroes don't compromise.

                    MECHLEY
(SADLY)
     Richard, I'm afraid you don't know the
     difference between a hero and a fool.

Deadeye gets up and moves toward Mechley,
whose back is to the door. We see Deadeye over
Mechley's shoulder.

                    MECHLEY
(TENSING)
     What are you doing?

                    DEADEYE
(STOPS A FEW FEET FROM MECHLEY)
     I'm leaving.

                    MECHLEY
     Richard, you might as well face facts.
     You're going to have to stay here for a
     while. This is...

                    DEADEYE
     Mechley, listen. There's somebody
     standing right behind you, ready to hit
     you over the head as soon as I give the
     signal.

Mechley frowns and raises his eyes at Deadeye's
foolishness.

     Now, since you're actually a pretty
     decent guy, Mechley, I'm gonna give you
     a choice. If you promise to step out
     of the way and let me leave this place
     without causing a ruckus, I'll tell the
     guy behind you to leave you alone.

     But if you insist on being stubborn...

                    MECHLEY
(IGNORING DEADEYE'S THREAT)
     Richard, go on back over and sit down.

MECHLEY (CONT'D)

I've got a little sensitivity game we
can play. I'll...

DEADEYE

(SHRUGS)

Okay, Mechley, it's your head.

(GIVES ORDER)

Let him have it.

There is a loud thud and Mechley drops to the
floor, out cold. Another angle shows Benny, who
has smacked Mechley on the head with a bedpan.
Benny is impressively dressed in buckskin; and
he is wearing the beaded headband from the Indian
booth in Red River.

Nice work, Benny! (INTRIGUED) How did
you find me here?

BENNY

All Indians know how to track.

Deadeye looks at Benny, a splendid figure in his
buckskin outfit, and smiles with delight, as they
move to exit from the room.

Deadeye stops and looks down at Mechley, still
unconscious on the floor.

DEADEYE

By the way, Mechley, I do know the dif-
ference between a hero and a fool. A
hero wins.

EXTERIOR MOVING TRAIN—DAY

A freight train is rolling west. Angle on boxcar
which carries Deadeye and Benny, unseen, inside.

> DEADEYE (VOICE OVER)
>
> How's Star?

> BENNY (VOICE OVER)
>
> Fine. Rainey promised to take care of
> the horses.

CUT TO:

INTERIOR BOXCAR—DAY

Deadeye and Benny are enjoying the ride. Deadeye
is flipping a silver dollar.

> BENNY
>
> You know this scar on my neck?

Deadeye stops flipping the coin and looks at
Benny.

> When I was eight-years-old, I tried to
> hang myself.

> DEADEYE
> (STUNNED, RUBS HIS OWN NECK)
>
> Why would you do that?

> BENNY
> (THINKS, THEN SHRUGS)
>
> I don't know.

160.

A moment of silence. Then Deadeye holds up his
coin.

                         DEADEYE
          See this silver dollar?

Benny nods.

          Watch.

Deadeye tosses the coin into the air, forms a gun
with his thumb and forefinger, and aims.

          Ptew!

The coin drops, Deadeye picks it up, and there is
a hole dead center!

                         BENNY
     (AGAPE)
          How did...?

Deadeye holds up a second silver dollar, one
without a hole in it.

                         DEADEYE
     (SMILING DEVIOUSLY)
          All you need is two silver dollars.

Benny suddenly realizes how Deadeye tricked the
Sheriff in Red River.

                         BENNY
     (LAUGHS)
          Oh-h-h, Deadeye...

DEADEYE

Oh-h-h, Benny...

DEADEYE AND BENNY (TOGETHER)
(CISCO AND PANCHO STYLE)

Ha ha, ha ha, ha ha ha!

They laugh uncontrollably.

DISSOLVE TO:

EXTERIOR RED RIVER—DAY

Main Street. Deadeye and Benny are being reunited
with their horses. Rainey is there. Deadeye is
making a fuss over Star.

DEADEYE

Hey, Star, how've you been? Did you
miss me? (PATTING HIM AFFECTIONATELY)
You're looking great, boy!

RAINEY

Deadeye...

Suddenly, over Star's saddle, Deadeye spots
Bulldog, Spike and a third Cowhand ride into
town, hitch their horses to a post, and enter the
saloon.

DEADEYE
(EXCITED)

Rainey, see those horses over there
(POINTS)?

Rainey does.

162.

DEADEYE (CONT'D)

Don't let 'em out of your sight.

(TO BENNY)

C'mon, Benny, let's get the Sheriff!

EXTERIOR RED RIVER—DAY—MOMENTS LATER

Deadeye leads Benny, Rainey and Sheriff Carter
to the three horses. Reaching into his pocket,
Deadeye takes out a piece of broken horseshoe and
hands it to the Sheriff.

DEADEYE

Hold this a minute, Sheriff.

The Sheriff, while making clear his skepticism,
takes the horseshoe piece.

Deadeye lifts up the right hind leg of Spike's
big brown horse.

It is wearing a full horseshoe. Surprised,
Deadeye quickly moves to the horse's left hind
leg and picks that up. That foot is also perfectly shod.

DEADEYE

They fixed the shoe!

The Sheriff looks at Deadeye, disbelieving, and
hands back the horseshoe piece.

SHERIFF

Do yourself a big favor, Deadeye. Don't
bother me anymore.

The Sheriff turns and heads back to his office. Foiled, Deadeye hurls the horseshoe piece to the ground in anger.

                    DEADEYE

     Goldangit!

(DETERMINED)

     I'm gonna nail those rustlers yet!

                    RAINEY

     Well, after today you won't have to
     worry about the rustling on our North
     Pasture, cowboy.

                    DEADEYE

(PUZZLED)

     Why not?

                    RAINEY

     Dad finally decided to sell.

                    DEADEYE

     Sell?

                    RAINEY

     Gordon Braxton's been offering to buy
     that land for a long time. Dad...

                    DEADEYE

     Braxton?!

164.

                    RAINEY
(SURPRISED AT DEADEYE'S REACTION)

     Yeah. He's out at our place right now
     closing the deal.

                    DEADEYE
(EXCITED)

     Of course! I had the wrong plot! They
     don't want the cattle, they want the
     land!

Deadeye turns and runs to Star. With a flying
leap, Deadeye lands perfectly in the stirrup and
on the saddle.

     C'mon, Star!

Deadeye and Star race out of town towards the
MacPheeters ranch.

EXTERIOR MacPHEETERS RANCH HOUSE—DAY

Scotty MacPheeters and Gordon Braxton are
sitting on opposite sides of a small wooden table
on the porch of the MacPheeters ranch house.
MacPheeters' shillelagh is propped against the
table on his side.

MARK ARMBRUSTER, Braxton's lawyer and aide,
is standing at Braxton's side. MacPheeters is
looking over some papers.

EXTERIOR OPEN COUNTRY—DAY

Deadeye is racing on horseback, heading for the
MacPheeters ranch.

EXTERIOR MacPHEETERS RANCH HOUSE—DAY

MacPheeters, Braxton and Armbruster on porch.

MacPHEETERS
(EXAMINING PAPERS)

Everything seems to be in order.

EXTERIOR OPEN COUNTRY—DAY

Deadeye is riding hard over hill and dale.

EXTERIOR MacPHEETERS RANCH HOUSE—DAY

MacPheeters, Braxton and Armbruster on porch.

MacPHEETERS

That land's been in my family for a
long time, Gordon. I really hate to see
it go.

BRAXTON

Nothing is forever, Scotty. Besides,
I'll take good care of it for you.

EXTERIOR RANCH LAND—DAY

Deadeye is racing desperately against the clock.

EXTERIOR MacPHEETERS RANCH HOUSE—DAY

Armbruster hands MacPheeters a pen.

EXTERIOR RANCH LAND—DAY

Deadeye is riding hard. The MacPheeters ranch
house is in sight.

EXTERIOR MacPHEETERS RANCH HOUSE—DAY

MacPheeters looks at the deed in front of him and prepares to sign. Deadeye can be seen on the horizon, and the sound of Star's galloping hooves causes the three men on the porch to stop and look up.

Deadeye comes riding up in a cloud of dust and hops off Star.

> DEADEYE

Don't sign that, Mr. MacPheeters!
Braxton is out to hoodwink you!

> ARMBRUSTER

(TO DEADEYE)

Hoodwink?

> BRAXTON

What are you talking about?

> DEADEYE

You know darn well what I'm talking
about. You hired Spike and some others
to rustle cattle from Mr. MacPheeters.
You figured you'd keep forcing Mr.
MacPheeters to lose money so that he'd
finally have to sell the North Pasture.

> BRAXTON

This guy's nuts.

                    MacPHEETERS

Deadeye, what makes you think Gordon
had anything to do with the rustling?

                     DEADEYE

Just give me two days to get the proof I
need. Promise me you won't sign anything
for at least two days. That's all I ask.

MacPheeters, confused, pauses to think.

                     BRAXTON
(ANNOYED)

    Is this some kind of a joke, Scotty? Do you
    actually believe what this jerk is saying?

                     DEADEYE
(TO MacPHEETERS, PLEADING)

    Just two days.

                     BRAXTON

This is crazy.

                    ARMBRUSTER
(TO DEADEYE)

    Do you realize you're interfering with
    a very important business deal?

                     BRAXTON
(TO DEADEYE)

    Listen, friend, if I weren't a peace-
    able man...

168.

                    MacPHEETERS
(GIVING IN TO DEADEYE)
     Well, I've waited this long to sell...
     I guess...

                    BRAXTON

     Scotty, I thought we had a deal?

                    MacPHEETERS

     Gordon, what's two more days? If
     there's nothing to what Deadeye here
     is saying, then there should be no
     problem, right?

Braxton and Armbruster exchange glances, not sure
how to respond.

(TO DEADEYE)

     Okay, Deadeye, you've got two days.

(TO BRAXTON)

     After that, Gordon, the land is yours.

                    DEADEYE

     Thanks, Mr. MacPheeters. You won't be sorry.

                                   DISSOLVE TO:

EXTERIOR RANGE LAND—DAY

Deadeye and Benny are ambling along on horseback.

                    DEADEYE
(DEEP IN THOUGHT)
     We've got two days to solve this thing, Benny.

They ride in silence for a few moments. Benny
finally speaks.

                    BENNY

    Have you, uh, have you noticed anything
    different, Deadeye? About my language,
    I mean?

                    DEADEYE
(STILL DEEP IN THOUGHT)

    What?

                    BENNY

    My language. (PROUD) You know, I don't
    say those words anymore.

                    DEADEYE
(MORE ATTENTIVE)

    What words?

                    BENNY

    You know, man, like fu...

                    DEADEYE

    Oh, oh yeah...those words. Yeah, Hey,
    that's great, Benny. I did notice that.
    And I'm really proud of you, too.
    You're a first-rate sidekick.

Benny smiles. As they pass by a large rock,
Deadeye and Benny are jumped and knocked from
their horses by two COWHANDS wearing ban-
danas to cover their faces. Using gun handles,
the Cowhands knock both Deadeye and Benny
unconscious.

EXTERIOR CABIN—DAY

Exterior shot of a ramshackle cabin, hidden off the beaten path. Star, Lizard and three other horses are hitched outside.

INTERIOR CABIN—BACK ROOM—DAY

Deadeye and Benny are seated on the cabin floor, their hands and feet bound with rope.

A Cowhand with a bandana over his face enters through a door that leads to the front room of the cabin. He looks at Deadeye and Benny.

                        COWHAND

     You finally came to, huh? Well, don't
     be alarmed or nothing. We just thought
     we'd invite y'all up to this cabin for
     a little vacation.

                        DEADEYE
(SARCASTIC)

     Gee, thanks. We appreciate it.

                        COWHAND

     Good place to rest and relax for a
     couple days, don't you think?

                        DEADEYE

     How much is Braxton paying you for
     this?

The Cowhand chuckles, then turns and leaves the
room.

INTERIOR CABIN—FRONT ROOM—DAY

The Cowhand closes the door to the back room and
pulls his bandana down to reveal his face. It is
Spike. Seated at a table in the room, playing
cards, are Bulldog and a third Cowhand. Some hol-
stered guns are hanging in the far corner. Spike
moves back to his seat at the table.

                        BULLDOG

     Are they awake?

                        SPIKE

     Yeah.

                    SPIKE (CONT'D)
(CHUCKLING)

     He asked how much Braxton was paying us
     for this.

                    BULLDOG

     Who, Deadeye?

                    SPIKE

     Yeah.

                    BULLDOG
(CONCERNED)

     There's something about that dude that
     really eats at me.

                    SPIKE

     What do you mean?

                    BULLDOG

     I don't know... Sometimes I get the
     weirdest feeling he's a...a CIA agent
     or something.

Spike and the other Cowhand laugh.

                    SPIKE

     You serious?

                    BULLDOG

     Well, you gotta admit he ain't your
     average guy.

                    SPIKE

    'Course not. He's crazy.

INTERIOR CABIN—BACK ROOM—DAY

Deadeye and Benny tied up. Benny maneuvers to lift his feet in the air, and a long knife drops from his boot to the floor.

                    DEADEYE
(SURPRISED)

    Where did you get that?

                    BENNY

    All Indians carry knives.

INTERIOR CABIN—FRONT ROOM—DAY

The three Cowhands are engrossed in their poker game.

INTERIOR CABIN—BACK ROOM—DAY

Deadeye and Benny are back to back. Benny is using his knife to cut the ropes from Deadeye's wrists. As they struggle with the ropes, they watch the door.

INTERIOR CABIN—FRONT ROOM—DAY

Bulldog shows his cards.

                    BULLDOG

    Aces and eights. Dead man's hand.

Smiles and collects his chips.

INTERIOR CABIN—BACK ROOM—DAY

Deadeye's ropes are off, and he is cutting the ropes from Benny.

INTERIOR CABIN—FRONT ROOM—DAY

Bulldog is dealing. There is a noise in the back room.

                    BULLDOG

    You better check on those guys, Spike.

Spike gets up, pulls his bandana up over his face, and moves to the door. He opens the door and looks inside the back room. The ropes are on the floor and Deadeye and Benny are gone. Spike sees the open window across the room.

                     SPIKE

    They're gone!

Angle on the cabin's front door. Deadeye and Benny come busting in. They lift up the poker table, knocking Bulldog and the other Cowhand to the floor, and a fight ensues.

Deadeye and Benny are both fighting furiously. The three Cowhands fight back, but they're taking a hell of a beating. Benny has subdued the third Cowhand by knocking him over the head with a chair. Finally, an exhausted Bulldog manages to knock Deadeye down.

                    BULLDOG

(TO SPIKE)

    Come on, let's get outta here!

EXTERIOR CABIN—DAY

Bulldog and Spike scramble out the front door of the cabin. They grab their horses and head for the hills.

INTERIOR CABIN—DAY

Deadeye gets up. He sees the third Cowhand lying on the floor, out cold.

                    DEADEYE
(TO BENNY)

        He's not going anywhere. Let's go after
        the other two!

EXTERIOR CABIN—DAY

Deadeye and Benny come running out the front door of the cabin. They hop on Star and Lizard and ride out after Bulldog and Spike.

EXTERIOR HIGHWAY—DAY

Bulldog and Spike ride out of the woods and come upon a highway. They stop, look around, then ride across the highway and disappear up over a ridge. A FARMER driving a haybaler watches them.

Deadeye and Benny come riding from the woods and stop at the highway. The Farmer on the haybaler calls to Deadeye and Benny.

                    FARMER
(POINTING UP OVER THE RIDGE)

        They went thattaway!

Deadeye and Benny quickly ride across the highway and up over the ridge.

176.

EXTERIOR OPEN LAND—DAY

Bulldog and Spike are riding hard. Deadeye and
Benny are giving chase. As Deadeye and Benny gain
ground, Bulldog and Spike split up and head in
different directions.

                    DEADEYE
(POINTING AFTER SPIKE)
     You take him, Benny!

Benny follows Spike, and Deadeye heads out after
Bulldog.

Riding hard, Benny catches up with Spike. He
rides alongside and jumps Spike, pulling him from
his horse. Benny and Spike fight.

EXTERIOR WILD COUNTRY—DAY

Deadeye is hot on Bulldog's trail. Hooves pound
and dust swirls as Deadeye and Star gain ground.

Approaching some rocks, Bulldog quickly dismounts, grabs his rifle from his horse and climbs
up into the rocks. Deadeye rides up, Bulldog
fires at him, and Deadeye quickly dives from Star
and takes cover behind some rocks. Deadeye tries
to spot the whereabouts of Bulldog in the rocks
above; and a couple bullets bounce off the rock
near Deadeye's head, forcing him back.

EXTERIOR OPEN LAND—DAY

Benny outfights Spike, finally subduing him.
Benny then grabs a rope from Spike's horse and,
with Spike lying face-down on the ground, brings
both of Spike's hands behind his back and begins
to efficiently tie his wrists.

EXTERIOR ROCKS—DAY

Bulldog is crouched behind a rock, rifle cocked, waiting anxiously for Deadeye to reveal himself below. Suddenly, there is a noise off to the side and Bulldog turns. He sees a hat—Deadeye's hat—moving slowly behind a big rock just a few yards away.

Bulldog smiles and waits for Deadeye to get to the end of the rock and appear in the open. As Deadeye's moving hat reaches the end of the rock, Bulldog aims and prepares to fire.

Out from behind the rock walks a stray COW, wearing Deadeye's hat.

                    COW
     Mooooooo...

Deadeye appears on a rock directly above Bulldog and jumps down on him, knocking the rifle from Bulldog's hands. Deadeye and Bulldog slug it out. And after a grueling battle, Deadeye finally manages to flatten Bulldog.

Deadeye leans against a rock to get his breath, then moves to get his hat back from the cow. As he does, Bulldog comes to.

He sees the rifle lying on the ground nearby, and starts to reach for it. Bulldog gets his hand on the rifle and is just about to pick it up, when a knife sails right through the rifle's trigger guard, fastening the gun to the ground.

Bulldog looks up and sees a smiling Benny. Deadeye turns and sees what has happened.

                    DEADEYE
     Nice work, Benny.

Benny moves to pick up the knife and rifle.

178.

                    DEADEYE (CONT'D)
Where's Spike?

                        BENNY
Tied to a tree.

Deadeye, with his hat back on, picks Bulldog up
by the shirt collar.

                       DEADEYE
Come on, Bulldog. Let's go get your two
friends.

                       BULLDOG
(EXHAUSTED)
What are you gonna do with us?

                       DEADEYE
I'm making a citizen's arrest.

INTERIOR BRAXTON'S OFFICE—DAY

                       BRAXTON
(SHOCKED)
A citizen's arrest?

Braxton is in his classy, Western-style office
at the Braxton Investment Company. Armbruster has
just come in. Both are standing.

                      ARMBRUSTER
They're locked up over at the jail now.

                    BRAXTON
They haven't talked, have they?

                   ARMBRUSTER
Not yet.

                    BRAXTON
Well, make sure they don't. Promise
them whatever they want!

(THINKS, THEN POUNDS HIS FIST ON THE DESK)

Damn it!

                   ARMBRUSTER
Deadeye called MacPheeters too; and
MacPheeters agreed to hold off on the
land deal for at least another week.

                    BRAXTON
That goddam Deadeye...

                   ARMBRUSTER
We're gonna have to get rid of him,
Gordon. There's no other way. The
people in this town are gonna start
thinking he's another Tom Mix or
something.

                    BRAXTON
(THINKS)

Yeah. We'll get rid of that lunatic,
all right! I'll call Ennio and have him
send somebody up here.

180.

INTERIOR MacPHEETERS RANCH HOUSE—DAY

Deadeye, Benny, Scotty MacPheeters and Rainey are
in the living room.

MacPHEETERS

I still find it hard to believe Gordon
Braxton would stoop to rustling cattle.

DEADEYE

He knew that's the only way he could
force you into selling your land.

RAINEY

(SKEPTICAL)

But why does he want the land that
badly?

BENNY

Maybe there's oil.

DEADEYE

(SNAPS HIS FINGERS)

Oil! That's it! There's oil on your
property!

RAINEY

There's no oil on this land.

MacPHEETERS

And even if there were, how would
Gordon know about it?

Pause, as Deadeye stands and moves across the
room. He stops, thinking intently.

> DEADEYE

There's some reason Braxton wants that
land; and we've gotta find out what it
is.

EXTERIOR RED RIVER—DAY ·

Deadeye exits from the front door of the Sheriff's
Office and moves down the sidewalk. He notices
Squirrely motioning to him from across the street,
and he hurries to Squirrely. Deadeye and Squirrely
are standing at the entrance to an alley.

> DEADEYE

What's up, Squirrely?

> SQUIRRELY

(ANXIOUS)

I've been keeping an eye on Braxton
like you asked me to.

> DEADEYE

Good. Have you found out anything?

> SQUIRRELY

(LOOKS AROUND NERVOUSLY TO MAKE SURE NO ONE
IS WATCHING THEM)

I heard 'em talking—Mr. Braxton and
that other guy...

> DEADEYE

Armbruster?

                    SQUIRRELY

          Yeah, him. I heard 'em say something
          about a "hit man" coming from Cheyenne.
          I think they're planning to have you
          killed, Deadeye.

                    DEADEYE
(REACTS, THINKING)

          So they've hired a gunslinger, huh? The
          Cheyenne Kid.

Squirrely looks at Deadeye quizzically.

          Ever heard of The Cheyenne Kid,
          Squirrely? They say he's fast. Very
          fast.

                    SQUIRRELY

(CONCERNED)

          What are you gonna do, Deadeye?

                    DEADEYE

          Only one thing I can do, Squirrely.

(THINKS)

          I've gotta be faster.

INTERIOR SILVER DOLLAR SALOON—DAY

Some PATRONS are drinking. Deadeye and Benny
enter through the swinging doors and move to a
door in the back of the saloon.

INTERIOR BACK ROOM OF SALOON—DAY

Six well-dressed MEN, including Braxton, are
seated at a table playing poker. A few other MEN

are scattered around, watching. Deadeye and Benny
enter. They stand off to the side and watch.
Deadeye stares intently at Braxton as the Men
play. Braxton finally lays down his cards—an ace-
high flush—and rakes in the pot. There is a large
amount of money and chips in front of Braxton. He
is obviously winning.

As the deal passes, Braxton notices Deadeye
staring at him.

                    BRAXTON
    You want something, Deadeye?

                    DEADEYE
(MOVES TO BRAXTON)
    Yeah, I want to leave a message with
    you.

                    BRAXTON
    A message?

                    DEADEYE
    Yeah. Tell The Cheyenne Kid I'll be
    waiting for him.

                    BRAXTON
    Who?

                    DEADEYE
    The Cheyenne Kid.

                    BRAXTON
(LAUGHING)
    Who the hell is The Cheyenne Kid?

184.

                         DEADEYE
          Tell him to start saying his prayers.

                         BRAXTON
     (SHAKES HIS HEAD. TO OTHER PLAYERS)
          This guy's nuts.

     (TO DEADEYE, FACETIOUSLY)
          Okay, I'll give him the message, Lone
          Ranger. Now beat it. We're trying to
          play cards.

                         DEADEYE
          I'm leaving.

Braxton reacts, relieved.

          Just as soon as you give those players
          their money back.

Braxton looks at Deadeye, disbelieving.

          You were cheating. Give 'em their money
          back.

                         BRAXTON
     (A BIT FLUSTERED)
          Cheating? What are... What makes you
          think I was cheating?

                         DEADEYE
          Your kind always cheats.

Benny moves next to Deadeye.

BRAXTON

(TO OTHER PLAYERS)

I told you he was nuts.

Benny is casually holding his knife, making sure
Braxton sees it.

BENNY

If you wanna make it outta here in one
piece, man, you better do what Deadeye
says. Give the money back.

Braxton pauses and looks at Deadeye and Benny.

BRAXTON

Okay, listen, you two. I don't want to
start any trouble in here, so I'll tell
you what. Let's settle this fair and
square. You say I was cheating, and I
say I wasn't. I'll make a deal with you.

(TO ANOTHER PLAYER)

Art, give me a deck of cards.

ART, a slender man with a vest, hands a deck to
Braxton.

(TO DEADEYE)

I'll bet you I can cut this deck and
cut the Jack of Hearts on my first try.

Deadeye and Benny exchange looks.

DEADEYE

If you don't cut the Jack of Hearts,
you'll give those men their money back?

186.

                         BRAXTON
          That's right, everything I won. But if
          I do cut the Jack of Hearts, you gotta
          promise me you and your buddy here will
          leave Red River by sundown and not come
          back.

(BEAT)

          What do you say, Deadeye? Is it a deal?

Deadeye considers.

                         DEADEYE
          Okay, Braxton, it's a deal.

Deadeye picks up the deck of cards.

          I'll shuffle.

He looks at the cards, shuffles them, then sets
them back on the table.

          Okay, cut the Jack of Hearts.

Deadeye and Benny watch carefully.

                         BRAXTON
(TURNS TO BENNY, WHO IS HOLDING HIS KNIFE)
          Could I borrow that for just a second?

Braxton takes Benny's knife and slams it down
through the entire deck of cards. The knife
is sticking through the deck and in the wooden
table.

(VICTORIOUS)

          If you look through the deck, I think
          you'll find that I cut the Jack of Hearts.

(SMILES)

>   Guess you'll be leaving town tonight,
>   huh, Deadeye?

Deadeye opens his hand and holds up a card.

                         DEADEYE
>   Fraid not, Braxton.

Deadeye shows Braxton the Jack of Hearts. Braxton
is flabbergasted!

(NODDING TOWARDS POKER TABLE)

>   You've got some money to return.

Braxton reacts, defeated.

EXTERIOR GUN SHOP—DAY

We see Deadeye through the window of a gun shop
in Red River. He is trying on a classy, rhine-
stone-studded two-gun holster as a SALESMAN
behind the counter looks on. A couple other MEN
are browsing in the shop.

INTERIOR GUN SHOP—DAY

Deadeye is adjusting the holsters. Each holster
has a leg strap tied firmly around Deadeye's
leg. The holsters fit him perfectly. The Salesman
behind the counter reaches into a glass case and
brings out two revolvers. He sets them on the
counter and Deadeye picks them up.

                         SALESMAN
>   They're the best pearl-handled six
>   shooters I've got.

Deadeye twirls them and sets them backwards in his holsters, Bill Elliott style.

> Those are fancy-looking guns. Make you
> look just like a cowboy movie star.

EXTERIOR RED RIVER—NIGHT

Establishing shot of Red River at night. The streets are practically empty. Live country-western music is playing somewhere in the distance.

EXTERIOR TOWN HALL PATIO—NIGHT

The music is louder now. It's coming from inside the Red River Town Hall, where a Wild West Days dance is taking place. Deadeye and Rainey have moved from the dance floor—visible through the open doors behind them—to the outside patio. They are standing alone near a wall at the edge of the patio. Rainey is dressed for the occasion in a Western gown.

Deadeye unwraps a stick of Doublemint gum and puts it in his mouth. He offers Rainey a piece, but she shakes her head "No."

They both stare out into the big, star-lit Wyoming sky. Deadeye takes a deep breath, then exhales.

190.

                    DEADEYE
          Nice night, isn't it?

Rainey nods. She is in a pensive mood.

          You know, a lot of people say that
          spring ls their favorite season. And
          other people like autumn, because of
          the leaves and all... And I guess some
          people even like winter best. But my
          favorite season is summer. I love this
          time of year.

     (BEAT)

          I guess it goes back to when I was
          a kid. Summer was the only time you
          really felt free, you know. The only
          time you didn't have to worry about
          school.

                    RAINEY
          You think a lot about when you were a
          kid, don't you?

                    DEADEYE
          Doesn't everybody?

Beat. They stare out into the night.

          You know, I wonder what it is that
          happens to you between the time you're
          a kid and the time you grow up. I mean,
          you're the same person, really. And
          you're living on the same planet.

                    RAINEY
          Things change.

                         DEADEYE
(THINKS)

     You know what I miss most about being a
     kid?

Rainey looks to Deadeye for the answer.

     Heroes.

Beat.

     Roy Rogers, Gene Autry, The Cisco Kid,
     Johnny Mack Brown, Hopalong Cassidy,
     Red Ryder, The Lone Ranger... There
     were so many heroes you had to keep
     sorting 'em out—deciding on your
     favorites, second favorites, third
     favorites. They fought against every
     kind of injustice. And they always won.

                         RAINEY

     Heroes only win in the movies.

(THINKS)

     In real life, heroes get shot.

EXTERIOR RED RIVER—NIGHT

A shadowy FIGURE is standing in an alley,
waiting. He is dressed in modern Western garb,
including dark boots, dark hat and a dark frock
coat.

Suddenly another FIGURE appears in the alley,
behind the Man in the dark outfit. The second
Figure moves toward the first Figure from behind.
He makes a slight noise, and the first Figure
reels quickly, reaching inside his coat as he

192.

does so, pulling out a semi-automatic pistol
and pointing it directly at the second Figure.
The second Figure freezes. We see that it's Mark
Armbruster.

                    ARMBRUSTER
          Hey, take it easy.

                     HIT MAN
          Don't go sneaking up on me like that.

                    ARMBRUSTER
          I wasn't sneaking up on you. I just
          don't want anybody seeing us.

The Hit Man puts his gun away. He carries it
hidden inside his coat in a holster which hangs
across the left side of his chest.

Armbruster moves to the Hit Man and hands him an
envelope.

          Here.

The Hit Man checks inside the envelope, thumbing
through a stack of bills and pulling out a photo.

          Everything is there.

                     HIT MAN
          (STUDYING THE PHOTO)
          Is this the guy?

                    ARMBRUSTER
          Yeah, that's him. He calls himself
          "Deadeye."

The Hit Man smiles.

Long shot of the two Figures from Squirrely's POV. Squirrely has been standing hidden in a doorway across the street, watching.

INTERIOR DANCE HALL—NIGHT

Deadeye and Rainey are standing on the dance floor. A large sign which says: WELCOME TO RED RIVER WILD WEST DAYS HOEDOWN is fixed high up on the wall. Focus on the bandstand, where a five-man country-western GROUP is arranged. The music has stopped and the band's LEADER steps up to the microphone.

                    LEADER
    Ladies and gentlemen, on this next
    number, the Ramblers are proud
    to feature Mr. Benny Selma on the
    harmonica.

There is some polite applause as Benny steps forward. Deadeye and Rainey applaud and watch the bandstand with interest. The Ramblers start playing and singing "Red River Valley," with Benny accompanying on harmonica. Everyone starts dancing, including Deadeye and Rainey. Benny's playing is great. Rainey pulls Deadeye close.

There is a verse break in the song and Benny goes into a harmonica solo. His playing wows the crowd.

                    MAN
(TO HIS WIFE)
    That Indian sure can play the
    harmonica!

194.

Benny's solo ends and the band's Leader begins
singing the final verses to "Red River Valley."
Squirrely appears at the door of the dance hall
and comes inside. Deadeye glances toward the
door and Squirrely catches his eye. When the song
ends, Rainey and Deadeye finish dancing and the
crowd goes wild with applause for Benny. Benny is
proud and pleased.

Deadeye leaves Rainey for a moment and moves to
Squirrely. Rainey watches as Squirrely and
Deadeye talk. Deadeye leaves Squirrely and comes
back to Rainey.

                    DEADEYE
(TO RAINEY)

    You wait here, Bobcat. I'll be back in
    a bit.

                    RAINEY

Where are you going?

                    DEADEYE

There's something I have to take care
of.

196.

                    RAINEY

        Deadeye, can't you stop playing cowboy
        just for tonight?

Deadeye looks at her.

        Stay here with me and relax.

                    DEADEYE

        I'd like to, Bobcat.

(BEAT)

        Really. But...

                    RAINEY
(REALIZING SHE CAN'T CHANGE HIS MIND)
        I know, I know—'What would your fans
        think?'

Deadeye looks at Rainey again, then turns to
leave.

EXTERIOR RED RIVER—NIGHT

Star is standing alone, hitched to a post.
Deadeye approaches, pats his horse, and opens
Star's saddlebags. He reaches into the saddlebags
and pulls out his pearl-handled revolvers and
holsters. He begins to strap them on.

EXTERIOR RED RIVER—NIGHT

The black boots of the Hit Man are squeaking
methodically as they move along the wooden sidewalk of a deserted Red River street.

EXTERIOR RED RIVER—NIGHT

Deadeye ties the leg straps of his holsters and moves in front of Star. He adjusts his holsters, loosens his pearl-handled guns, then drops his arms, preparing for a practice draw.

Deadeye nervously stretches his fingers, stiffens, then cross draws. He fumbles. He gets his guns out, but the draw is not fast. Deadeye sweats. For a second, a look of fear seems to flash across his face.

He puts his guns back, and prepares to try again. This time his draw is extremely swift and accurate. He smiles confidently, twirls his guns impressively and puts them back in their holsters. He looks into Star's face, smiles, and hugs his horse. Star whinnies approvingly.

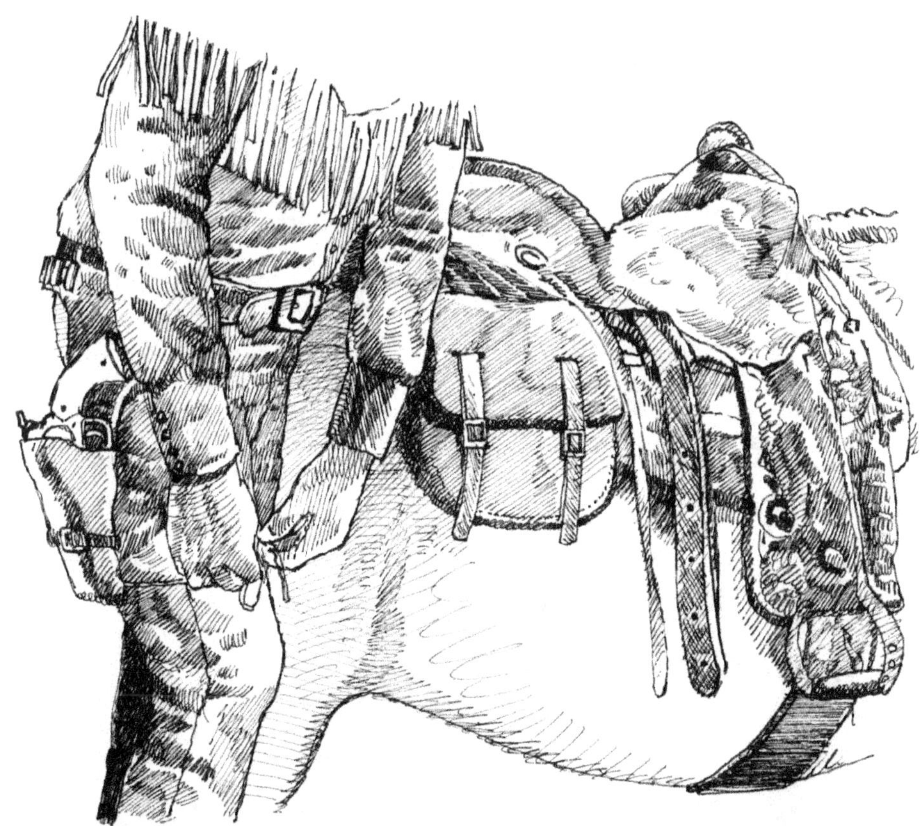

EXTERIOR RED RIVER—NIGHT

The Hit Man walks casually to a street corner, then turns left and moves towards the music, in the direction of the Town Hall.

Deadeye's POV.

Deadeye sees the Hit Man walking in his direction, on the opposite side of the street. Deadeye begins walking towards the Hit Man. When the two figures come to within a hundred yards of each other, Deadeye steps out into the street and calls to the surprised Hit Man.

> DEADEYE
>
> You looking for me?

The Hit Man stops, silent for a moment.

> HIT MAN
>
> Who're you?

> DEADEYE
>
> Deadeye.

The Hit Man steps into the street to get a closer look at Deadeye.

> HIT MAN
>
> What makes you think I'm looking for you?

> DEADEYE
>
> You're The Cheyenne Kid, aren't you?

The Hit Man stands fast, silent. Deadeye smiles.

You didn't expect me to be waiting for
you, did you, Kid?

Deadeye inches closer.

                    HIT MAN

Why don't we go somewhere and talk?

                    DEADEYE

What's there to talk about? You came
here to kill me, didn't you? Well, make
your move.

                    HIT MAN

Look, Wyatt, I ain't even carrying a
gun.

                    DEADEYE

Yeah? What's that inside your jacket?

The Hit Man reacts.

     A concealed weapon, huh? You got a
     license to carry that?

Benny has appeared at the end of the street.
Squirrely is behind him, on the sidewalk.

Deadeye inches toward the Hit Man. The Hit Man
realizes he's not going to be able to talk his
way out of this. He tenses up and moves farther
out into the street. He stops and faces Deadeye.

Deadeye stops. Both men face each other, staring
hard. They prepare for a confrontation.

                    HIT MAN

Okay, Wyatt. I'll play your game. Let's
see how fast you really are.

200.

                    DEADEYE
          I'm waiting on you, Kid. Whenever you
          feel lucky.

Angered by Deadeye's brashness, the Hit Man makes
his move. They draw, Deadeye's guns come out
lightning fast. Ptew! Ptew! The Hit Man's gun is
out and he fires. Deadeye drops.

A shocked Benny comes running to Deadeye and
kneels down beside him.

                    BENNY
          Deadeye! Deadeye!

Deadeye's eyes are open. There is blood on his
shirt.

          You beat him, Deadeye! You outdrew him!

In anger, Benny picks up one of Deadeye's guns
and turns toward the Hit Man. Benny aims and
pulls the trigger, but the hammer just clicks. He
pulls again and again, but the gun doesn't fire.

                    BENNY
     (STUNNED)
          Deadeye! You forgot the bullets!

The Hit Man has moved closer to Deadeye. He aims
his semi-automatic at Deadeye and prepares to
finish him off.

There is a loud SHOT; and the Hit Man drops his
gun and falls to the ground—dead. Standing alone
at the end of the street is Sheriff Carter,
holding his smoking gun with both hands.

Some PEOPLE have started to arrive on the scene.
Benny props Deadeye's head up.

                    BENNY
(TEARS IN HIS EYES)
     Talk to me, Deadeye... Please, talk to
     me!

People begin to encircle Deadeye.

Deadeye's POV: among the cowboy boots in the
Crowd is a pair of black WING TIP SHOES. The
camera pans up to show the Private Eye from
Minneapolis.

Deadeye turns his eyes to Benny.

                    DEADEYE
(STRUGGLING TO SPEAK)
     Make sure they bury me with my boots
     on, Benny.

                    BENNY
(FIGHTING BACK THE TEARS)
     You ain't gonna die, Deadeye. You
     can't! You and me got lots of adven-
     tures left!

The Sheriff moves into the Crowd, pushing a few
People aside. Deadeye looks up and sees the
Sheriff.

                    DEADEYE
(STILL STRUGGLING AS HE SPEAKS)
     And make sure they bury me here—in Red
     River.

Rainey appears on the sidewalk, and runs into the
street. She moves to Deadeye. Their eyes meet.
Rainey is stunned.

202.

She wants to cry, but she can't. Somehow, she knew all along it would end this way.

Deadeye tries to speak, but his face winces in pain.

                    DEADEYE
        Shit...

Deadeye's body goes limp, and he falls back in Benny's arms.

The Sheriff, Rainey, Squirrely, the Private Eye and others look on as the camera pulls back for a high shot of Main Street, showing the small Crowd gathered around Deadeye.

                              DISSOLVE TO:

INTERIOR SHERIFF'S OFFICE—LATE DAY

The Sheriff is at his desk. Seated across from him, shillelagh in hand, is Scotty MacPheeters.

                    SHERIFF
        I did some checking on that pasture
        land of yours, and it seems Deadeye was
        on to something after all. The state is
        planning to run a new freeway through
        there.

                    MacPHEETERS
(SURPRISED}
        A freeway?

                    SHERIFF
        Yep. I followed up on another hunch,
        too, and found out that Braxton and

some businessmen from back East have
been planning to build motels and
restaurants all around here. They've
been scheming to turn Red River into a
tourist resort.

The front door opens and the Private Eye from
Minneapolis enters. He moves to the Sheriff and
produces a piece of paper.

PRIVATE EYE

Okay, Sheriff. Here's a wire from his
sister authorizing me to take the body
back to Minneapolis.

The Sheriff takes the paper and studies it.

She's got her lawyer's name and
number there, in case you've got any
questions.

The Sheriff smiles and hands the paper back to
the Private Eye.

SHERIFF

I just got one question—'When are you
leaving Red River?'

PRIVATE EYE
(DETERMINED)

As soon as you give me custody of
Richard Wentworth's body.

SHERIFF

Well, in that case, Mr., uh...

204.

                    PRIVATE EYE

        Adams.

                      SHERIFF

        In that case, Mr. Adams, you're gonna
        be here for a long, long time.

                    PRIVATE EYE
        (PROTESTING)

        Sheriff...

                      SHERIFF
        (ANNOYED)

            Look, Adams, I'm only gonna tell you
            one more time. In this town, a man's
            dying request means something. Now
            Deadeye asked to be buried in Red
            River. And as long as I'm Sheriff here,
            his body's gonna stay right where it
            is—buried in our cemetery.

EXTERIOR CEMETERY—LATE DAY

Tight shot of a fresh marble tombstone which
reads: RICHARD W. WENTWORTH BORN JUNE 27, 1946
DIED JULY 24, 1977 R.I.P.

Pull back to show Benny standing in front of
the tombstone, staring. Lizard is saddled and
standing off to the side. This is the Red River
cemetery, a small graveyard cluttered with old
tombstones and located on a slope just outside of
town.

A pickup truck pulls to a stop on the dirt road
alongside the cemetery. Rainey and Squirrely

climb out of the truck and approach Benny. Rainey
is holding a bouquet of forget-me-nots.

Rainey sets the flowers at the foot of Deadeye's
grave, and the three stand in silence for a
moment. A train whistle BLOWS in the distance.
Benny turns and moves to Lizard.

                    RAINEY

          Are you sure you don't wanna stay
          around for a while, Benny?

Benny, looking splendid in his buckskin outfit,
mounts Lizard.

                    BENNY

          Thanks anyway, Rainey. But me and
          Lizard gotta move on. Bye, Squirrely.

                    SQUIRRELY

          Good luck, Benny.

Squirrely and Rainey wave as Benny rides off over
the ridge silhouetted against the Western sky,
with "Red River Valley" (featuring harmonica)
playing over the scene.

On the other side of the ridge, Benny goes into
a gallop and is startled as a horse and rider
suddenly appear from behind some brush. It is
Deadeye and Star! Benny stops, speechless.

                    DEADEYE
(SMILING)

          Hiya, Benny!

                         BENNY

(ASTOUNDED)

    Deadeye! Wha... Are you a ghost?

                        DEADEYE

(LAUGHS)

    Naw, I'm not a ghost.

(EXPLAINING)

    The Sheriff and I made a deal. He
    wanted me out of town; and I wanted my
    sister off my tail.

                         BENNY

(TOTALLY CONFUSED)

    But what... How...

                        DEADEYE

    Sorry I didn't let you know sooner. But
    I couldn't take any chances on being
    seen.

                         BENNY

    But... Didn't you get shot?

                        DEADEYE

(RUBS HIS SIDE)

    Ah, it was just a scratch.

                         BENNY

    But who's buried back there?

DEADEYE

(SMILING)

The Cheyenne Kid.

Benny reacts, still a bit bewildered. Deadeye
rears his horse and starts to ride off.

C'mon, Benny, let's go! Maybe we can
reach the next town before sundown.

Benny watches Deadeye ride off, then finally
starts after him.

BENNY

(CALLING)

Hey, Deadeye, wait for me!

Benny rides hard to catch up with Deadeye,
finally does, and, with an upbeat version of "Red
River Valley" playing over the scene, the two
ride off into the sunset.

THE END

ABOUT THE AUTHOR

Jay Moriarty is a writer who lives in Los Angeles.

Also by Jay Moriarty:

HONKY IN THE HOUSE
Writing & Producing The Jeffersons

The author with his childhood heroes.

www.ingramcontent.com/pod-product-compliance
Lightning Source LLC
Chambersburg PA
CBHW061206210726
48294CB00006B/1775